DETROIT PUBLIC LIBRARY

3 5674 05697018 0

CHANDLER PARK LIBRARY
12800 Harper Ave.
Detroit, MI 48213

Lil Mama From The Projects 3

By: Mz. Toni

D1713938

FEB - - 2019

Copyright © 2016 Mz. Toni

Published by Tiece Mickens Presents, LLC

All rights reserved. No part of this book may be reproduced in any form without prior written consent of the publisher, excepting brief quotes used in reviews.

This is a work of fiction. Any references or similarities to actual events, real people, living or dead, or to the real locals are intended to give the novel a sense of reality. Any similarity in other names, characters, places, and incidents are entirely coincidental.

Acknowledgements

I want to dedicate this book to my baby sister Janaya Lynch my angel gone too soon. Every book I write is for you R.I.P

Writing this book was so bittersweet for me, I honestly didn't want it to end I want to thank everyone who supported me, whether you purchased a copy, shared a link, changed your profile picture, if you did anything to help it is greatly appreciated. I want to thank my mom for being so awesome and supporting me, I love you mommy! I want to thank my awesome test readers Terina Wright and Shana O'gilvie, Shana you irk my whole soul but in the end we make a great team. I want to thank Tyanna Coston my sister from another mister, thank you for sharing links, being genuinely supportive, and for being a listening ear for all my crazy stories. To my hubby, thanks for pushing me, supporting me and keeping your bad son out of my way so I can get some writing in, I love you babe. To my family from Jersey to Brooklyn who have supported me, thank you all.

To all my loyal, amazing and patient readers who patiently and non patiently waited for my book, I love you guys to the moon and back for rocking with me so hard. Shout out to my Sis Corrie, you were one of the first people to read this, thanks for being honest, and thank you for being a true friend, you get on my nerves but I love you. Shout out to Kellz

Kimberly, Yasmine Davis, Briana Millz, and my whole TP, MMP, TMP,RWP Family the support is real and always appreciated. To Tiece Mickens, you are so genuine and kindhearted that it's hard to just see you as a boss, thank you for continuing to be strong even in adversity, nobody said being the boss was easy but you make it look good! To Ebony Lawdddddd thank you for being honest, always keeping it a milli and never steering away from your true self I love that about you the most. To the editor thanks for doing an amazing job in my opinion the editing is the most important part, so you are definitely appreciated.

Chapter One (Cherish)

It's been four months since I got the tape and almost killed Mega and his little girlfriend. Since then, things have been close to perfect. I'm still going to therapy and growing as a woman more and more every day. Me and Mega are co-parenting our beautiful twins and things have been going great. I don't entertain him and I don't converse with him unless it's pertaining to our children. My eighteenth birthday is a week away and I have been so busy planning our trip to the Bahamas and taking care of the twins that even if I wanted to talk to that nigga, I wouldn't know where or how to find the time.

"Hello Ms. Daniels, I am taking the twins to the park," my nanny said with a smile. Evelyn was a huge help, especially since I had been working on starting a business. I had just moved into my new four-bedroom home and after some discussion, I decided to move her in. She was great with the kids and had grown to be like a mother figure to me. I wasn't one of those parents that left my children with the nanny often, but she was a big help.

"That's fine, Ms. Evelyn," I said before getting up and giving my babies all the kisses. When she left, I decided to go out as well. Getting in my car, I headed to the mall to try and find my babies more things that they really didn't need. Plus, I wanted to buy a few more things for my birthday vacation. While walking from store to store, I heard a familiar voice call out my name. Turning around, I was surprised to see Peter, the realtor that had helped me find my condo.

"Hey Cherish!" he said with a handsome smile.

"Hey Peter, how you been?"

"I've been good. But I'm even better now that I'm seeing you," he said, causing me to blush.

"Yeah, it's been awhile," I said with a smile. While we were talking, a little boy who looked to be five, rushed over to him, grabbing his leg. He was followed by a beautiful white woman, who I assumed to be his wife.

"I was wondering where you rushed off to," she said to Peter. I don't know why I felt uncomfortable, but I did, and I wanted to leave as quickly as possible.

"Well it was nice seeing you Peter, take care," I said, before turning to leave.

"Wait, Cherish!" he said, stopping me.

"I didn't know you had a son, and is that your wife?"

"No, no hold on," he said, before calling the woman and little boy over to us.

"What are you doing?" I asked in a whisper.

"Diana, this is Cherish. Cherish, this is my sister Diana and nephew Luke," he said.

"Oh hi, this is the infamous Cherish," she said with a smile.

"He's mentioned me?" I asked her.

"Most certainly," she said, giving me a wink.

"We were just going to Chili's for lunch, would you like to join us?" he asked.

"I don't want to impose," I said.

"Nonsense. I've been trying to find you for a while now, and now that I have, I'm not gonna let you go that easy."

"You two go, me and Luke here are going to Chuck E. Cheese," his sister said before walking away with her son in tow.

"So I guess it's just you and me," he said, grabbing my hand. When we arrived to Chili's, which was next to the mall, we were quickly seated and he wasted no time asking me questions.

"I see you're not pregnant anymore."

"Oh no, I had them seven months ago," I said with a smile.

"Congratulations on that."

"Thank you."

"I thought you were running from me, especially when I found out you moved."

"Noooo, I needed more room after having the twins."

"So are you still in a bad spot?"

"Not at all. I'm actually the happiest I've ever been."

"Things worked out with you and your man?"

"Yes, we parted ways. It hurt at first, but I got over it."

"That's good. So can I take you out again?"

"I would love that. I'm going to the Bahamas in a couple days, but when I get back, I will call you," I said, pulling out my phone and taking his number. For hours, we ate and talked about how life had been for us these past seven months, and I was happy to find out that he was still very single. I also found out that he was the top realtor in his company at the tender age of twenty-three, he had no children, had never been married, and he was just as handsome as I remembered.

"I wouldn't mind going on a vacation with you," he said jokingly.

"Maybe next time," I said with a laugh. There was no way in hell I was bringing a man with me to the Bahamas. I wanted to let my hair loose and for the first time, have fun without a care in the world. After paying the bill, he walked me to my car and for the first time in a long time, I was nervous as hell.

"I had a lot of fun with you Cherish."

"I enjoyed spending time with you too," I said with a smile. Leaning towards me, he gently grabbed the back of my neck and pulled me in for a kiss. Lawd, when I say this man kissed me with so much passion and lust, he had me weak at the knees. We kissed for over five minutes before I realized that a little goodbye kissed had turned into a full make-out session in the middle of the mall parking lot. Pulling back, I hurried and got into my car before I changed my mind. As I drove home, all I could do was smile, while thoughts of him took over my mind.

Chapter Two (Mega)

"Hey baby, you hungry?" Kaliah asked me when she walked into my office.

"Yeah, a little. Why, you cooking?"

"No, I was gonna order something," she said.

"Naw, I'm good," I replied.

I was so tired of eating fast food or at restaurants, the shit was annoying as hell. I had gotten used to Cherish cooking a home cooked dinner almost every night, and Kaliah didn't cook at all. When everything went down that night, the moment Cherish walked away, I knew I had fucked up, but I also knew it was too late. Maybe I went about shit the wrong way. Maybe I should have given Lil Mama some time. She was pregnant, hormonal, young, and on top of that, she had been through a lot. It seems like she's mentally moved on from me. Even though she doesn't have a man, she also doesn't show interest in me or what I do.

I don't even know how me and Kaliah happened, it started off as something to do. Me and her had an understanding, but before I knew it, we were spending all of our free time together and she was calling herself my girl. She's a cool ass chick, but she ain't wifey material. For some reason, I don't vibe with her like I did Cherish. I'm seeing a lot of shit that Cherish used to do that Kaliah doesn't, and that shit is fucking with me. The sex is off the chain. She ain't new to the shit, but that's the only area she's a pro in. You would think a woman of her age would know more about cooking, cleaning, and overall how to treat a man, but she doesn't.

"Are you coming to bed?" she asked, snapping me out of my thoughts. Looking at my watch, I saw that it was three in the morning.

"Yeah, I'm coming soon?" I said nonchalantly.

"What's up with you Jason?"

"What you mean?"

"I don't know. You been acting real fucking funny style."

"Man, ain't nothing wrong with me."

"Whatever, I don't care."

"That's the problem, ya ass don't care about shit!"

"Nigga, I don't care about shit, you really feel that way?"

"I'm used to my girl doing shit like cooking. Shit, you ain't gotta clean my shit, but at least clean up ya shit," I said, shaking my head.

"You want me to do shit like I'm ya girl, but you don't treat me like ya girl!"

"How you figure? You damn near done moved in."

"I haven't even really met ya daughter. Whenever you have her, I can't come around. You don't let me around the twins, and I haven't met anyone in ya circle either."

"I don't have a fucking circle. You ain't seen my kids since the shit popped off cuz I ain't tryna disrespect Lil Mama!"

"Do you see a future with me, because I'm confused on how this is gonna work out. We're gonna be married, but I can't see ya kids?"

"Woah, slow down, ain't nobody say shit about getting married."

"What the fuck, Jason? I don't understand what you want from me."

"I want you, Kaliah. I have feelings for you."

"When I met you, I didn't want or expect anything from you, but now I'mma need you to give me something Jason." "I'm sorry babe," I said, hugging her. I needed to face the fact that me and Cherish weren't right for each other and move on.

"I forgive you, but I need to see change," she said before walking out. Grabbing my phone, I called Cherish.

"What's up?" she answered.

"Can you talk?" I asked.

"Yeah, go head."

"I wanted to know how you felt about my girl being around the kids."

"I don't care Mega. As long she doesn't bring any harm to them, I'm straight," she said nonchalantly.

"So, just like that?" I asked confused.

"Just like that," she said, hanging up in my ear. I couldn't do shit but shake my head. She wanna be a mature adult right now, but where the fuck was this side of her when she had a gun pointed in my face. Walking upstairs, I was stopped by an alarm going off outside. Rushing out the front door, I knew Kaliah was gonna be pissed when she saw this shit.

"What the fuck!"

"I know, I'mma get it fixed," I said, while looking around.

"Oh, these bitches got the right one. I'm bout to call my cousins, you know where these hoes live!" she snapped, pulling out her phone.

"Yo, chill out, I'll handle this shit," I said, calming her down.

"You fucking better before I take matters into my own hands!" she screamed while walking back into the house. I swear if it wasn't one thing it was another, a nigga just couldn't catch a break. I wasn't going into another relationship just so those crazy bitches could ruin it. Going upstairs, I stopped in Jasmine's room to tuck her in, before taking my ass to bed. I don't even remember falling asleep, but I remember being woken up.

"Babe, wake up, the police are downstairs!" Kaliah said.

"What!" I said, jumping up and running downstairs.

"Hello Jason Cruz, I'm Officer Carter. I'm here on behalf of Ashley Jones, who states that you kidnapped her child."

"I did what? Jasmine is my daughter and Ashley left her with me almost three years ago."

"I'm sorry, but unless you have proof, I need you to go get her and hand her over to the mother," he said sympathetically. As I looked over his shoulder, I could see Ashley and Jayda standing by the cop car. Ashley looked as if she didn't really want to be doing this, but that he/she Jayden had the biggest smile on his face. Pulling out my phone, I called Cherish to let her know what was going on. I didn't want her to bring Jasmine over, but I felt like Cherish needed to know what was going down.

"I do have proof," I said with a smirk.

"He's lying. I didn't get any custody papers!" Ashley snapped. Ignoring her, I walked into the house and straight into my office. After getting what I needed, I walked back outside and handed the officer the appropriate paperwork.

"Ma'am, he has full custody of your child."

"How is that possible!" Jayda screamed.

"Bitch, you ain't got shit to do with what they got going on!" Kaliah snapped at Jayda. With her hands on her hips, she walked over to Jayda, as if she was ready to fight.

"Neither do you. Mega, you better get this bitch out my face. She don't even know who she fucking with!"

"Oh bitch, I know you a nigga, and I'll still dog walk ya faggot ass all up and down this driveway. Y'all hoes wanna be fucking up cars and shit!" Kaliah snapped. Rushing over to them, I pulled Kaliah back and had to carry her into the house. When I came back out, they were still outside with the police.

"I don't understand how a judge could just give him my child," Ashley said, on the verge of tears.

"You left her on my doorstep with nothing. I had no number to call you and neither did the judge. He sent papers to all of your last known addresses and he gave you time to come and you didn't."

"I wish I could help, but he has everything needed to prove that he has custody of the said child, so there's nothing I can do," he said sympathetically, before getting into his squad car and leaving.

"I just wanna see my daughter," she said, as the tears finally fell from her eyes.

"You should've thought about that before you just up and left your child," Cherish said. I turned around and there she was, looking sexy as hell with her scarf and sweat pants on.

"What is this bitch even doing here?" Jayda asked.

"I got ya bitch, bitch!"

"I thought I told you that you didn't need to come," I said, pulling Cherish to the side.

"I know what you said, but when bitches come around with the cops tryna take my child, I'mma be front and center!"

"Your child?" Ashley whispered.

"Look, I know you gave birth to her and I don't doubt that you love her, but I'm almost certain this shit ain't about her," Cherish said calmly.

"I do love her!"

"Well if you love her, you would know and understand that she's best with us. Can you give her what she needs, what she wants? If not, you're being selfish as hell right now!" Cherish snapped.

"Cherish is right!" Kaliah said. This chick was like a magician. I had just put her in the house and already she had managed to slip back outside. When Kaliah spoke, everyone was silent, including Cherish. This was her first time seeing Kaliah since the night she found out about us and punched her in the face, I just knew when they saw each other again it would be a problem, so I braced myself for a fight.

"Ain't you the bitch that was fucking with Mega while he was with this bitch!" Jayda screamed, while laughing.

"Man, you over here tryna start fucking trouble with ya faggot ass. Get the fuck from my house before you leave in a body bag!" I snapped.

"Jason, don't say shit to JAYDEN's gay ass. I ain't worried about him or the shit that went down, I'm over it, my only concern is my kids," Cherish said honestly. As much as I wanted to applaud her maturity, part of me was feeling a little jealous that she was over me so fucking fast.

"I don't want to fight, I just want to see my baby. I know I fucked up, but I'm trying to make things right."

"Maybe she can have supervised visits," Cherish said.

"She gotta leave that shim at home. As long as she does, then I'm cool with her stopping by," I said, giving in.

"Thank you so much, Jason, and thank you Cherish!" she said happily.

"No problem. Call me tomorrow so we can set something up," I said, before watching them get in their car and leave. When they were gone, Kaliah walked up to me and Cherish and I knew what she was going to do, so I just watched and waited to see what Cherish's reaction would be.

"Listen Cherish, I've been meaning to talk to you. Seeing how you said you were over it, I thought—".

"Please don't think that just because I'm over the shit, that I've forgotten. Yes, I've grown, but ain't all the growth in the world gon make me forget about what y'all did," Cherish said after cutting her off. When she was done, she turned around and walked to her car without so much as a goodbye, and pulled off.

Chapter Three (Cherish)

I can't believe that bitch thought that she could come up to me with some bullshit apology. I let that shit go, not for them, but for me. Being angry was taking too much damn energy. I'm so tired of being angry and bitter about the shit, so as much as I wanted to slap the shit out of her on site, I chose to let it go. When I got back home, I undressed and hopped in the shower. Seeing them together was a little stressful for me. When he called me earlier, asking if the kids could see her, I wanted to curse his ass out for even suggesting some shit like that. Over the past few weeks, Peter, me and the kids had been doing a lot of thing together, along with his adorable nephew, so I didn't want to be a hypocrite. Yeah, we had been seeing a lot of each other since our run in at the mall. I liked him a lot, but to be completely honest, I was miserable without Mega and I felt it was time to get my man back. After showering, I took my ass to sleep. I had school tomorrow and on the days I went, they were my longest days of the week, so I needed to be well rested.

The next morning, I woke up bright and early. I had barely slept last night because I was so nervous about actually talking to Mega and telling him how I felt, but as nervous as I was, I needed to be a grown woman and let him know my true feelings, before it was too late. After getting the twins ready, I dropped them off with Mega, only to have Kaliah tell me that he had gone to go handle some business, so she would be watching them until he came home. Yes, I know I told him it was cool if they were around her, but shit, I didn't mean she could watch them and shit. I would definitely be having a talk with him about this later. I had every mind to just keep them, but I couldn't afford to miss any days, especially since I would be going on vacation soon. Pulling off, my next stop was dropping Jasmine off at school. When that was done, I headed straight to class. I loved school and I was doing exceptionally well in all my classes. I was going for business, and had plans to open up a teen outreach program/shelter for teens with nowhere to go. I was lucky and found a way out, but most kids like me don't find that and are left to fend for themselves in this cold, cruel world. I wanted to create a sanctuary for them. I haven't told too many people, but I recently purchased the perfect building. Well, Camille did, since I wasn't at an age to put anything in my name. The building needed some work, but Mark referred me to some contractors who could get the job done in no time. All I needed was for my eighteenth birthday to hurry up and come. When I got into my car, my phone started ringing. Looking down, I noticed it was Mega and quickly answered.

"What's up Lil Mama?" he asked, as soon as the call connected.

"Nothing, we need to talk."

"I know. I shouldn't have made you leave the kids with Kaliah. It won't happen again, but I had an emergency," he explained.

"Yeah, I was gonna cuss ya ass out, but I need to talk to you about something else."

"Is it important, because I have a busy week."

"No, it can wait, just let me know when you're free," I said.

"Aight, I got you. I gotta go, I have a meeting in a few minutes."

"Ok, bye," I said, hanging up. Damn, I thought I would be able to get the shit over with, but I guess it wasn't meant to happen now. I definitely wasn't rushing it, so I would just have to wait. As soon as I hung up with him, I got another call from Peter. When I answered the call, I could hear him singing some pop song that I'd never heard of.

"Hello?" I said, laughing.

"How are you beautiful?" he asked.

"I'm good, how are you?"

"Great, now that I've heard your voice," he replied, causing me to smile. He was so damn corny, but I liked it.

"So, what you got planned for today?"

"Nothing much, trying to see you."

"I have a lunch date with Camille, but I'm all yours after that," I said. After hanging up with Peter, I drove to the Cheesecake Factory to meet up with my girl. Walking into the restaurant, I spotted Camille and quickly walked up to her.

"Girl, I gotta talk to you," she said.

"What you done did?"

"Man, so I went home and I'm like babe, you gotta watch the kids cuz me and the girls going to the Bahamas for Cherish's birthday. Before I know it, he done invited himself and called all the guys."

"I don't care, I'm single."

"I thought I was gon turn up," she said with a pout.

"Bitch, you shoulda known Mark wasn't letting ya hot ass go out of the country alone," I said laughing.

"Well, you can bring ya lil sexy white boo. I mean shit, y'all going strong."

"Naw, I don't want to invite him. We ain't been dating long enough to be going on vacations and shit," I said, turning up my nose.

"You think you fooling somebody. You just don't want Mega to know you took him," she said laughing.

"Bitch, you tried it. I don't care what Jason knows!"

"Uh huh!"

"Seriously though, I'm gonna tell him I'm ready to work on us," I said.

"Wait, tell who, Peter?" she asked.

"No, Jason."

"Oh shit, my baby growing up. You better go get ya man," she said with a smile. While eating lunch, we talked about everything under the sun. From the kids, to the outreach program, to school. I had a lot going on and she never once missed a time to tell me how proud she was of me.

"So did you call that contractor?" she asked.

"Yeah, I called. They are coming this weekend to check it out and give me an estimate."

"Are you excited?"

"Hell yeah. I've always wanted to help people and this is my chance."

"Well, you know how proud I am of you and I'm willing to help you in any way I can," she said sincerely.

"Thank you!"

"Aight, well I gotta head out. I'm going to see Shante and my godson."

"Ok, I'm meeting up with Peter anyways, so call me," I said, hugging her. After we parted ways, I drove home so I could meet Peter there. The kids were staying the night with Mega, so we would be alone for the first time in weeks. Pulling up to my house, I didn't see Peter's car anywhere, so I took advantage of that and went to go hop in the shower and throw something comfortable on. As I stood in the shower and as the suds ran down my body, I couldn't help but think of Mega and how much I missed him. As I was stepping out the shower, I heard a light knock at the door. Grabbing my robe, I fastened it tightly around my body and rushed to open the door.

"Well damn, what a great way to welcome someone!" Peter said with a bright smile.

"I thought I could shower and be dressed by the time you came," I said, laughing.

"You don't have to lie sweetheart. If you wanted me to see you all damp and sexy, just admit it," he said jokingly.

"Hush and get in here," I said, shaking my head and laughing. When he came in the house, I went to go get fully dressed. When I came back into the living room, he was staring at my pictures on the wall. There were some old pictures of me and Jason, and some pictures of Jason and the kids.

"Nice looking family," he said with a smirk.

"Oh don't tell me you're jealous," I said with a laugh.

"Who me, no never."

"Uh huh."

"So are you excited about the Bahamas, it's happening pretty soon."

"This will be my first time out of the country, so yes, I'm very excited," I said with a smile.

"How is the work on the outreach program going?" he asked, before wrapping his arms around me. That was one of the things I loved about Peter, he genuinely paid attention to me, he asked me questions and when I gave him answers, he actually listened to them.

"It's going good. I appreciate you finding that building for me. I just closed on it a few days ago, now I just have to meet with the contractors tomorrow for an estimate.""You're doing big things, aren't you? If you need me for anything, just know I'm here for you beautiful."

"Yeah, I'm trying, and thank you handsome," I said, kissing his cheek. After talking and watching a few movies, we both fell asleep on the couch. You would think with a nice, attentive and handsome man right next to me, he would be all I could think about, but honestly, as I laid beside him, my dreams were about Mega.

Chapter Four (Mega)

Things with me and Kaliah have been going better than usual, now that she was able to spend time with the kids. The twins love her, but Jasmine, not so much. I understand she's older and she is having a harder time accepting the fact that I'm with someone other than Cherish.

"Hey baby girl, you want to go to the park today?"

"Yes, can the twins come too?" she asked.

"Of course, now get up and get ready," I said, before walking out of her room and closing the door behind me. After me and Kaliah got the twins dressed and ready, we waited downstairs for Jasmine to come down and join us for breakfast.

"Why is she dressed?" Jasmine asked, staring at Kaliah.

"What you mean?"

"You didn't say she was coming!"

"Yo, fix ya tone!" I snapped.

"I don't have to go," Kaliah said sadly.

"You're going and that's the end of it!"

"Well, I don't wanna go anymore," Jasmine pouted.

"You're going too, so sit ya ass down, eat that cereal and fix ya face!"

"Why every time I come here I gotta eat cereal? What, she don't know how to cook?" Jasmine said with a smirk. It was then and there that I was fed up with her smart ass mouth.

"You tired of cereal, then don't eat at all. Take ya little grown ass upstairs!" I snapped. Standing up, she grabbed her bowl and dumped it in the sink, before heading upstairs. When I finally went to check on her, she was on the phone and had Cherish on speaker phone. Instead of making my presence known, I just listened.

"Jas, if ya dad wants to be with her, then you need to learn how to respect her."

"I just don't understand why he's with her when he has you."

"See, that's you being grown. It ain't ya place to understand why we aren't together. I'm sure you hurt her feelings and she deserves an apology."

"I'm not saying sorry to her, mom."

"Yes, you are. I'm not forcing you to apologize, but I know you'll do the right thing."

"Ugh aight mom, I'mma call you back."

"Love you Jazzy," she said, before hanging up. When she was off the phone, I ran downstairs and waited for her to say whatever she had to say.

"Sorry for being disrespectful," she said when she came downstairs. She still had an attitude and didn't really seem sincere, but I knew we would have to take what we could get cuz she had an attitude like that damn Cherish.

"It's ok baby. I know it's gonna take time for you to get comfortable with me, but I'm willing to work on it if you are."

"Well, you can still go to the park with us if you want to."

"Yeah, I would love to."

"Thank you for being you babygirl," I said, kissing Jasmine on the forehead. When we left for the park, we actually had a great time. Jasmine was a little anti-social, but she was on her best behavior overall. Looking at Kaliah interact with the kids, made me feel a different kind of way about her. Like, what the fuck was I doing, I needed to stop playing with her feelings and take the next step. Yeah, I love Cherish with all my heart, but I needed to think realistically. She was young and had a lot of growing to do. Here I had Kaliah who knew exactly what she wanted and how to get it.

When we left the park, I bathed the twins and put them to sleep, with the help of Kaliah. After Jasmine was showered and in the living room watching TV, I headed out to speak to someone I knew would keep it real. Pulling up to Mark's house,

I hopped out the car and knocked on the door, only to have Camille answer it.

"What you doing here?" she asked.

"I came to speak to my boy, where he at?" I said, pushing past her lightly.

"He's in the basement," she said, before walking upstairs. When I got downstairs, Mark was chilling with Kasan, Chris and Terrence, and the basement was filled with smoke.

"What's up?" I said, dapping each of them up.

"Ain't shit, what you been up to nigga?" Mark said.

"Man, I've been busy as shit with this record label taking off and shit."

"I feel you. So how you and ya girl doing?" "We good, that's kinda why I stopped by. Shorty cool and shit and she on her grown woman shit. I just think we need to take shit to the next level."

"The next level like what?"

"I wanna propose to her," I said honestly.

"Nigga is you stupid!" Kasan said, shaking his head.

"What you mean, shorty a fucking catch."

"So you ain't got no feelings for Lil Mama no more?"

"I love her, always will, but I can't keep on loving someone who ain't ready for my love. I might end up losing someone who's ready."

"I feel you. You just need to make sure that this is really what you want to do."

"I think it is."

"Aight then, I guess congratulations are in order," Kasan said, giving me a brotherly hug. We chilled, talked, smoked and drank. I was having a good time, until I got a phone call that I wasn't expecting.

"You good babe?" I asked, when I answered Kaliah's phone call.

"Naw, I'm not. Ashley and Jayda came here and took Jasmine."

"What the fuck you mean they took Jasmine!"

"Ashley came to the house and told me you said she could spend some time with Jasmine. I knew we had talked about it, so I didn't know what to do but tell her it was fine. After Jasmine was dressed and already in the car, that's when I noticed Jayda was in the backseat."

"Why would you let her take my daughter without my permission? You could've called me before she took her, just like you calling me now!"

"I'm sorry, damn. How was I supposed to know you didn't want her to go, after you clearly told me that you were going to start letting them spend time together? Nobody told you to leave, so while you pointing the finger at me, just think about that and the fact that if you were home with us, where you belong, then this wouldn't have happened!" she screamed. I could hear one of the twins crying, while I dapped my niggas and rushed home. When I got home, I jumped out the car. When I got to the front door, Kaliah was already waiting for me.

"I'm so sorry Jason!" she said with teary eyes.

"It's not your fault. Don't worry, I'mma get her back," I said, hugging her tight.

"Should we call Cherish?"

"No, ain't no point in worrying her yet," I said. As I stood pacing in my living room, I got tired of standing around not doing anything. Grabbing my gun, I got ready to walk out the door.

"Where you going?" Kaliah asked.

"I'm going to find my baby girl, fuck you mean!"

"I just don't want you to doing nothing stupid," she said, standing in front of the door.

"Get out my way!"

"Please Jason, think about your kids."

"I ain't thinking about my fucking kids? Do you know how dangerous that crazy bitch Jayda is!" I screamed. As we were arguing back and forth, I heard the knob on the front door turn and in came Jasmine with an ice cream cone, all smiles.

"Hey daddy!"

"Hey baby girl, you ok?" I asked, checking her over for marks or bruises.

"I'm fine, what's wrong?"

"Is everything ok? I just wanted to treat her to some ice cream and spend a little time with her," Ashley said. Giving her the look of death, I ignored what she said and focused on my daughter.

"Nothing, go upstairs and get ready for bed, it's late," I said. When Jasmine was upstairs, I wasted no time digging into Ashley.

"Who the fuck told you that you could stop by unannounced and pick up my daughter without my permission!"

"I didn't do anything, and we came right back," she said.

"I don't give a fuck. I told you to call me and I also told you not to have her around that crazy bitch Jayda!"

"I know, but she wouldn't let me go alone!" she pleaded.

"Wouldn't let you? Last time I checked, you're fucking grown!"

"I know. It was a stupid mistake and it will never happen again. Please don't take my baby from me." "Look, I ain't gon take her from you, but let's be clear. I need you to understand that I don't trust you or that bitch and if you want to see Jasmine, it needs to be supervised by me."

"I understand."

"I hope you do because if this shit happens again, then you won't be seeing her!"

"Ok, can I call you tomorrow and set up a meet?" she asked.

"Yeah, tomorrow is good Ashley," I said, while rubbing my forehead. I just needed her to leave. Seems like whenever this bitch was around, I got an instant headache. When she left, I looked at Kaliah and I knew I had fucked up. If looks could kill, a nigga would have been six feet under.

"What you cook babe?" I asked.

"Nothing."

"So it's obvious you mad at a nigga, so go head and talk so we can fix this shit."

"I have nothing to say to you!"

"Come on now, I know I snapped on you, but I was worried." "I don't give a fuck how worried you were, ain't nobody tell ya simple ass to knock up a simple bitch. If you're gonna take ya anger out on anybody, it should have been her ass!"

"Aight aight, my bad, damn," I said, putting my hands up to show her that I surrender.

"Yeah, ya bad," she said with an attitude. Before turning around to walk upstairs, following behind her, I walked into my bedroom and watched as she got her shit.

"What you doing?"

"I'm leaving, before I have to smack the shit out of somebody!"

"Who the fuck you slapping!" I snapped through gritted teeth.

"Jason, just leave me alone!"

"Man, I said sorry, damn!"

"You really don't get it, do you? Yeah you snapped on me and you shouldn't have, but that ain't even what I'm most mad about!"

"So tell me."

"Nobody respects me as ya woman. Jasmine don't, ya stinkin ass baby mama don't, and hell, neither do you!" "Fuck you mean I don't respect you!"

"I asked to spend time with your kids and you did that, and I appreciate it, but I ain't no damn baby sitter!"

"All I was doing was chilling with Mark and them. I wasn't even gone that long and I don't leave you with them any other time. Stop fucking acting like a child and tell me what's the problem!"

"How you know I ain't wanna chill with you and them? You never bring me to get togethers with them, I'm like some secret," she pouted.

"Yo, fix ya face. If I wanted to deal with a spoiled fucking child, I would have stayed with Cherish!" I screamed before I could stop myself. With a look of hurt, she raised her hand and slapped the dog shit out of me.

"How dare you compare me to her. You wanna be with her, then by all means do you cuz I'm out!" she said, before grabbing her shit and storming out the room.

Chapter Five (Ashley)

"I just don't understand how you can be so fucking stupid sometimes!" Jayda screamed, shaking her head.

"I'm not stupid, damn. I miss my baby and I'm tired of all this!" I snapped.

"All I asked you to do was grab the little brat. You claim to miss her, so I'm confused as to why you brought her back."

"I knew she would call Jason and I just want to go about things the right way."

"So what, you not with me no more?"

"I'm always with you, but aren't you tired of chasing after a nigga who obviously doesn't want you," I said, confused and tired.

"Bitch, who are you to say he doesn't want me? It's all these other hoes always in the way!"

"I ain't telling you nothing you shouldn't already see for yourself. You said Cherish was the problem, but they're not together anymore and he done found somebody else." "What the fuck? I know you act stupid, but you can't be this stupid. His friends know who I am, how would it look if he came with me on his arm?"

"That's really what you think?" I asked before laughing. I couldn't help it. I didn't see it before, but I see it now, this bitch is completely delusional.

"You laughing at me, you think I'm a fucking joke!" she screamed. Before I knew what was happening, she was already standing over me, pounding my body.

"Stop Jayda, I wasn't making fun of you!" I screamed, while trying to block my face. She had the strength of a grown man because at one point, she was. She was putting a hurting on me something terrible and I didn't know how to stop her.

"I'm so tired of everybody thinking I'm a fucking joke!" she screamed, while still hitting me.

"Jayda, stop!" I screamed, before using my foot and kicking her in the stomach and onto the floor. Jumping over her body, I rushed to the bathroom and closed the door, locking it behind me. As I looked in the mirror, I couldn't do shit but cry. How could she do that to me after all I've done for her? How could she hurt me like this? As I grabbed a washcloth out the closet and wet it with hot water, all I could think about is all the many times I've had to do this in the past growing up, and how I vowed never to have to do this again.

"Hey granny's baby," my grandmother said. I knew what she wanted, so I pretended to be sleep. I thought it had worked when I felt her get off my bed and when I heard my

bedroom door open. Getting up to close and lock my door, my grandmother opened it as I was locking it. The look on her face let me know just how my night would be.

"Bitch, you thought you could trick me!" she snarled before slapping me across the face and onto my bed.

"No, I wasn't trying to trick you, I swear!"

"So you gonna stand there and lie right in my face. Go get my switch!"

"I'm sorry, I'm just so tired," I said as tears fell from my eyes.

"You too tired for God!"

"No, but between school, housework, church and praying, I'm just so tired," I pleaded.

"Oh, so you just wanted me to cut some of your daily duties?" she asked with a smile.

"Yes please," I said innocently.

"Oh bitch, you think you special. Ya mama had to do everything you doing right now and she did it!" "No, I don't think I'm special!"

"Just in case you thought you were, bitch I'm here to tell you that you ain't!" she said, before walking out. When she came back, she had the switch with her and I knew this would be a long night. Taking off my nightgown, I grabbed the stool and got in the position I knew all too well. That night, Granny beat me for over an hour, and that next morning was the last time I saw my granny. When I got to school the next morning, my teacher walked by while she was teaching and noticed blood coming through the back of my shirt. She wasted no time calling me out the room and into the nurse's office. When I took my shirt off, they both broke down in tears at the bruises, scars and open wounds on my back.

"Who did this to you Ashley?" my teacher asked. I was so scared that I didn't say anything, I just stayed silent. My grandmother always told me that if I tried to tell anyone, no one would believe me. My grandmother was known as a God fearing woman who helped often in the community.

"You can tell us," the nurse said.

"My granny," I said quietly.

"Who?"

"My granny," I said louder.

"Oh my God. Ms. Evans did this to you?" "She's been doing this to me for five years, but I know you guys don't believe me. Just send me back to class and leave me alone."

"Ashley, I'm not the rest of this damn town. I don't put anyone on a pedestal that they don't deserve to be on. If you *said she did it, then I believe you," my teacher said, hugging me.*

"You do?" I asked, as tears fell from my eyes.

"Yes, why wouldn't I, the proof is right here. You couldn't have done that to yourself."

"So what happens now?" I asked.

"We call the police and DYFS," she said. When all was said and done, my granny was arrested and I was taken to my first foster home.

"Ashley, open the door!" Jayda screamed, bringing me back from my trip down memory lane.

"Leave me alone!'

"Come on, I'm sorry. I don't know what came over me," she said through the door.

"You beat me Jayda. Did you forget that you are a man with the strength of a damn man!" I snapped."I know, I know and I'm sorry. Just come out the bathroom so we can talk," she pleaded. I knew what I needed to do, I needed to leave and never look back.

"I love you Ashley, you're my best friend and all I got," Jayda said. Walking up to the door, I unlocked it. I know I must look stupid, but this was the only love I've ever had. Jayda treated me better than anyone I'd ever known. So what she got upset for the first time and got carried away.

"I love you too," I said, hugging her.

"I know I've been a little on edge, but I just need him to see how much I love him."

"Why be with someone who you have to do all this for? I'm here and I love you," I said sincerely.

"You're my friend and I love you. Maybe in another life we would have been soulmates, but I know in my heart that Jason is the one for me," she said.

"Well, I gotta go," I said sadly.

"Wait, where you going?" she asked.

"Jason said I can go hang with Jasmine today."

"Why didn't you tell me?"

"Because the only rule he has is that I can't bring you," I said honestly.

"Yeah, whatever. Well clean ya nose before you go," she said with a smirk. Rolling my eyes, I walked into the bathroom to clean myself up, and when I was done, I headed out to go see my baby girl. I know people think I'm not shit. I mean, what kind of mother leaves her child, but I had no choice. Everything I did was for her. I needed to get myself cleaned up and I needed to take care of myself. I knew I was no good to her in the condition I was in.

When I got with my boyfriend, I thought he was a godsend. He was good to me and he showed a lot of attention to Jasmine. He was so sweet and he took care of me, so when he introduced me to tricking, I thought shit, I could use the money and with him there to protect me, I knew I would be safe. I didn't realize that he had become my pimp until I stopped seeing the money that I was working so hard for. By the time I was smart enough to leave, he had got me strung out on coke. I always sniffed socially, but this shit was addictive and I had never had a high like it. I started losing weight, I barely saw my baby and tricking was the only thing I did. I hardly slept. One day I came home early because I was missing my baby something serious. When I walked into my bedroom, I watched as my daughter laid on my bed with no clothes on, while my so called man took pictures of her. Grabbing an E&J bottle, I held it tight and swung for his head. My intentions were to knock his head off, but because I was so small and so tired, I missed. That day we fought hard and after he beat my ass, he assured me that if I tried to take her, he would find us both and kill us. Apparently, he was making a lot of money selling my daughter's nude pictures to perverts online. I felt like shit. I was so busy getting high and fucking for money that I made my daughter become a victim. I felt horrible and I knew I had to make things right or my baby would never forgive me. So later that night while he was sleep, I grabbed my baby and took her some place that I knew she would be safe. When I dropped her off, I cried so hard and so bad, but I knew Jason would take care of her.

Pulling up to Jason's house, I grabbed a teddy bear that I'd bought for her the other day, fixed my clothes, and checked my makeup. When I knew I was right, I walked up to the door to knock.

"What's up Ashley?"

"Hey Jason, thanks for calling me," I said happily.

"I talked to Jasmine and she was excited about seeing you again. She's in the play room with the twins," he said, moving to the side and letting me in. Walking through his house, I was taken aback at how beautiful and big it was. I couldn't help but think that if I'd had a different life that maybe I would have been the one he chose and we would be raising Jasmine together. Walking into the playroom, I watched as his children sat in their walkers with bright smiles, as Jasmine gave them fake food and pretended to be a restaurant owner.

"Hey baby!" I said, surprising her.

"Hey Mama Ashley!" she said excitedly, before hugging me.

"I got you something!" I said, before picking the teddy bear up and handing it to her.

"Oh wow, a teddy bear," she said, not sounding too excited about it.

"Yeah, I know. You love to collect teddy's," I said with a smile.

"Thanks, I like it," she said. I felt like I was off to a good start. I bet she'd thought I forgot about how much she loved teddy bears, but little did she know, I remembered everything there was to know about my baby.

"You're welcome. Well, what are you playing, can I play?" I asked.

"I'm playing cooking. You can be another customer," she said, laughing.

"So, you like cooking?" I asked.

"Yeah, Daddy takes me to cooking classes twice a week. I'm getting really good, but Daddy says I can't cook alone because I might burn the house down, so I just play with this and pretend I made it," she said with a shrug.

"Maybe one day you can cook for me."

"What y'all doing?" Jason asked, walking into the playroom.

"Nothing, I'm cooking for Mommy Ashley," she said. It hurt me to the core to hear her call me that because I knew that meant she called Cherish mom.

"Oh ok, well I just came to grab the twins," he said, before picking the little girl up first.

"I can help you," I said.

"Naw, I got it, I'm used to holding both," he said, before grabbing the boy and walking out. We played and talked for two hours, before Jason said it was time for me to go. I wanted to be mad, but I wasn't. I was just thankful that he let me see her.

"Alright baby, I love you," I said, hugging her.

"Love you too, see you later," she said with a smile. Seeing Jasmine made me want to become a better me. I promise one day soon I'm gonna prove to everyone that I'm a good person and mother, despite my mistakes.

Chapter Six (Mega)

"So, did you enjoy spending time with Ashley?"

"It was ok, but a little weird."

"Why was it weird?" I asked.

"She doesn't know me anymore daddy. I don't like none of the things I liked before. She bought me a teddy bear, but I'm about to be a preteen, I don't want no teddy bears."

"Well at least she made an effort. She's been gone for a while, so she has to get to know you again."

"I know dad, I'mma try."

"Good, baby girl, but I wanted to run something by you."

"'Aight, what's up?"

"How would you feel about me proposing to Kaliah tonight?"

"I don't like her. I mean she cool, but I don't like her with you," she said honestly.

"Why, you don't think she good enough for me?" "Nope, I don't. Plus, we like to eat and she can't cook. I like mommy for you," she said with a smile.

"Jasmine, me and Cherish tried and it didn't work out, but we both deserve to be happy," I said.

"I understand. If you really love her daddy, then go ahead and propose."

"Thanks baby girl," I said, hugging my smart daughter. Getting up, I walked to my bedroom to get dressed. I knew I would need to go to her house since she refused to answer my calls. I didn't tell anyone, but I had gone with Mark and picked up the perfect ring to propose to her. He kept asking me over and over was I sure that this was what I wanted and honestly, I felt like it was. Getting the kids into the car, I drove to Kaliah's house. To say I was nervous was an understatement, a nigga was scared as hell. Pulling up to her house, I grabbed the kids and went to knock on her door.

"You look scared daddy," Jasmine said laughing.

"I ain't scared, little girl."

"Why you sweatin like that?"

"Mind ya business," I said, playfully mushing her in the head. Knocking on the door, I waited for her to answer. When she opened the door, she looked surprised to see us.

"Jason, what are you doing here?" she asked."We came because we miss you," I said with a smile.

"Can we come in at least?" Jasmine asked.

"Oh yeah, I'm sorry Jas, come on in," she said, while giving me the evil eye. When I walked into her house, I left the twins in their car seats and sat them on the couch, and Kaliah gave Jasmine the remote, so she could watch TV.

"I know you're pissed at a nigga, but I need you to come back," I said.

"For what?" she asked.

"Because I love you and the kids love you and I want to spend the rest of my life with you," I said, before getting down on one knee and pulling out the ring.

"Is that what I think it is?"

"Yeah, it is. I wanted to know if you wanted to be my wife?" I asked.

"And you're ok with this?" she asked Jasmine.

"Yeah," Jasmine shrugged.

"Yes, I'll marry you!" she screamed excitedly. Jumping into my arms, she kissed me passionately. Placing her back on her feet, I placed the ring on her finger."The crew and their women are going bowling, so I'mma go drop the kids off home and come through to scoop you afterwards."

"Ok, well have fun bowling," she said sadly.

"What you mean 'well have fun', you going with me!" I said, while laughing.

"Really, you're letting me meet them!"

"If you gonna be my wife, then I can't keep you away," I said, before kissing her and walking out the door. After getting the kids into the car, I called Mark to see what time they were heading out and to let him know that I was bringing Kaliah.

"What up nigga?" Mark said.

"Yo, what time y'all heading out?" I asked.

"We about to head out now. Why, what's up?"

"Shit, I'mma drop the kids off, then slide through."

"We bringing the girls, so you might as well bring your kids too."

"Aight, bet. Oh, and I'm bringing Kaliah too."

"Nigga, do you gotta death wish, you know how the women can be."

"I know. That's why I'm telling you now, so you can talk to your wife."

"Aight nigga, you asked for it," he said before hanging up. After he hung up, I called Kalliah and told her about the change of plans, and in ten minutes, she was outside, looking good and ready to go. When we pulled up to the bowling alley,

Kaliah was nervous enough for both of us, and I couldn't help but say a silent prayer that the women were on their best behavior. When we walked into the alley, I quickly spotted the crew. When we walked up to them, all the laughing stopped, as they gave me and Kaliah the evil eye.

"Hey god Mom!" Jasmine said, breaking the ice. Running up to Camille, she hugged her tightly.

"Hey baby, I missed you so much," Camille said.

"Bring me my babies!" Shante said with a smile. Since Kaliah was holding one of the car seats, she nervously and quietly walked over to Shante and handed her the car seat.

"Thank you. So what are you, the new nanny?" Shante asked.

"No, she's not the nanny Shante, she's my girl," I said, grabbing Kaliah's hand. I knew for a fact that Shante had met the kids' nanny before, so she knew that Kalliah wasn't it. All I could do was shake my head at her messy ass.

"Naw, she the homewrecker!"

"Come on, Camille. You know me and Cherish weren't even together when I met Kaliah," I said.

"Actually, I'm the fiancé," Kaliah said with a smirk, before holding up her hand and flashing her ring.

"I know you didn't Jason!"

"Come on now, let's not do this," Mark said, grabbing Camille's waist.

"You're right, let's have fun, but this shit ain't over," she said, rolling her eyes at me and walking away. The whole night was just awkward as hell. Kaliah basically sat in the corner the whole time, unless it was her turn to bowl.

"Are you seriously marrying that girl?" Camille asked.

"Yeah, I am, and I'm asking you not to tell Cherish."

"What you mean don't tell her, she deserves to know."

"I'm telling her tonight when I drop the kids off," I said honestly.

"Well as long as you tell her tonight, then we good. But come tomorrow, if she don't know, I'm telling nigga!" she snapped, before walking away.

"Y'all can be a little nicer to her too," I said, pissed.

"Nicer to who? That bitch ain't no friend of ours!" Camille said loudly enough for Kaliah to hear. Turning around, Kaliah looked at Camille and rolled her eyes.

"Oh, she a little feisty, huh," Shante said, laughing.

"Yeah, she is."

"Well tell her don't get too feisty before she gets these hands," Shante said with a smirk, before blowing Kaliah a kiss.

"Everything alright bro?" Kasan asked.

"Man, I'm bout to head out. They being real messy with my girl."

"Yo, what did you expect. They're loyal to Cherish, not her."

"I feel you," I said before walking away.

Chapter Seven (Cherish)

"So what do you have planned for today?" Peter asked me as he watched me get dressed.

"I got a busy ass day. I have to meet with the contractors, then head off to school. I have a big test that I can't miss because it's worth fifty percent of my grade. Then Mega is supposed to drop the kids off after school and I still have permits for the outreach program I have to apply for online. I still haven't even gone shopping for the Bahamas and I leave in two days," I said, feeling overwhelmed.

"Slow down. I can handle some of the business side of things, just give me a layout of what you want and need and I'll meet with the contractors for you today.

"Awwww thanks boo, but I got it," I said with a smile. I was so excited to be handling business on my own. It made me truly feel like an adult, so unless I had no choice, I was ok taking care of my own shit. After getting dressed, I headed out to my building to meet the contractors. Kissing Peter lightly, I watched as he got into his car and pulled off, and when he was gone, I headed out. When I pulled up to the building, I couldn't help but smile brightly at my hot mess, because I saw all the possibilities and that alone excited me.

"Hello, you must be Cherish. I'm Marcus Green and this is my partner Lamont Archer," he said, greeting me as soon as I walked up to the building.

"Nice meeting you both," I said with a smile. After unlocking the building, we all walked in and from the smile on their faces, I could tell they liked what they saw.

"Damn, this building is big. The structure is great in here."

"This right here, I want to be a day program for my teen outreach program," I said, talking about the first floor.

"Wow, that's great that you're doing something for the lost children in this world."

"I was a lot child myself not too long ago, so yeah, I want to help in any way I can."

"I feel you," he said, writing in a notebook."

"Ok, well let me walk you guys around so you can see the rest," I said as we stepped on the elevator to go to the second floor. As we got onto the elevator, I pressed the number two button and nothing happened. Clicking it a few more times, I realized that it just wasn't gonna work. "We will have that fixed in no time, but it doesn't look like this thing is gonna move, so maybe we should take the stairs," Lamont said, laughing.

"Maybe you're right," I laughed. Walking up a flight of stairs, we reached the second floor, which had so much potential. There had to be space for about fifteen rooms, maybe twenty, between this floor and the third, which was more than enough for me.

"So, what are you tryna do with this floor?" he asked.

"I'm gonna have the bedrooms for the shelter on this floor and the third floor," I said with a smile.

"So you would need a front office, a kitchen and an about twenty-five rooms, give or take?" he asked.

"Exactly!" I said, loving that we were on the same page.

"So when were you looking to have this done?"

"Asap. I'm going on vacation in a couple days for my birthday, and I would really like for it to be done within a month. I don't think it's bad, I really think it's possible."

"I mean, that sounds great, but it would take me and my men to be working on your place around the clock to get that done," he said honestly.

"Is that a problem?"

"Well that's gonna cost you."

"How much?"

"Well normally it would run you about fifteen thousand, but seeing as though you're doing a service to our community, I can do it for ten."

"No, I don't want any handouts. As long as you do an awesome job and have it running within a month, I'm willing to pay the normal price," I said, not wanting to owe anyone anything.

"Ok, whatever you want. I would need half to start immediately, and the other half when the job is complete and to your liking."

"Ok, that works," I said with a smile.

"Well, I have a contract for you to sign and then we can get started," he said, shaking my hand. After signing the paperwork, giving them a check and going over everything I wanted and needed to have, I locked the building back up and we parted ways. Looking at the time in my car, I realized I only had ten minutes to get to class so I could take my exam. Pulling off, I rushed out of the parking lot. As I was fast walking to class, I bumped into some girl, causing all her papers to fall to the floor. The look on her face told me she wasn't happy.

"I'm so sorry," I said, before bending over to help her pick up her things.

"Just leave it, I got it!" she snapped, before snatching a paper I'd picked up out my hand.

"I was just trying to help. You don't have to be nasty about the shit," I calmly snapped back.

"Why don't you just watch where you're going next time!" the girl said, before getting up and storming away.

"Cherish, why you just standing there, the test is about to start," one of my classmates said.

"I know, I'm coming," I said, before walking into class. When I was done taking the exam, I felt confident that I'd aced it. As I walked to my car, I saw someone leaning on my baby. As I got closer, I noticed that it was Peter.

"Hello beautiful!" he said with a smile.

"What are you doing here?" I asked, before hugging him.

"I was in the area and figured I'd take you out to lunch," he said.

"Ok, thank you. I guess I'll follow you," I said, kissing him lightly before getting into my car. When we pulled up to a diner near my school, we pulled in and parked. I didn't know why he met me at school, he had never done anything like that before. He usually called me to confirm and I liked it that way. I didn't need him getting too comfortable.

"So, I kinda lied," he said when we sat down.

"Lied about what?" I asked, confused.

"I wasn't in the area. I came because I wanted to talk to you."

"Ok, what's up?" I said.

"From the moment I first met you, I knew there was something different about you. You had this presence about yourself that made me want to know you on any kind of level. I didn't care, I was willing to take what I could get. Spending this time with you showed me that I don't want to spend time with anyone else. I understand that you have a lot going on, but I'm willing to take this ride with you if you'll allow me."

"Peter, you are a good man and I enjoy all the time we spend together, but it sounds like you're asking me to give you more than I can right now."

"Cherish, I'm not asking you to marry me, I'm just asking you to let me in."

"I like you so much, but you know I just got out of a relationship. I guess what I'm trying to say is I need some time to get to know me, before I allow you to sweep me off my feet," I said honestly.

"I understand and I'm willing to give you the time that you need, but just know I'm here," he said, reaching over the table to kiss me. When we were done eating, he paid the bill and walked me to my car. I felt bad for shutting him down, but I was so confused and right now, my heart was still with Mega. I refused to make things more confusing than they already were by adding someone else into the equation.

When I got home, I hopped in the shower and relaxed. Mega called me and said he would be dropping the kids off in a little while and that we could talk. I was nervous as hell, but ready to get it all out. I wasn't sure how he would take everything I planned on saying and honestly, I didn't care, I just wanted it to be out. My nerves started to get the best of me when I heard him pull up and park in my driveway. I could hear his speakers bumping, like always.

"Heyyyy mommy, I missed you!" Jasmine said, running full speed.

"Hey my baby girl, I missed you too."

"Daddy asked Kaliah to marry him and she said yes," she whispered before quickly running into her room. I didn't even know how to take what she had just told me. I felt like someone had just punched me in the gut and ripped out my heart. Quickly wiping my tears, I went to help him grab the twins. When he walked in, he placed the car seats on the floor and I did everything in my power not to look him in his eyes because I knew I would break down.

"I needed to talk to you about something. I know you've been trying to talk to me, so you go head first," he said before sitting down.

"It's nothing, I handled it myself," I said, looking down at the floor.

"You sure? I know I've been a little busy, but you know I got you if you need anything," he said sincerely.

"I know Jason," I said, while playing with my fingernails.

"Aight, but I needed to tell you something. I wanted to be the first person you heard it from."

"What's up?" I asked.

"I asked Kaliah to marry me," he blurted out.

"Congratulations, but I need to get the kids ready for bed, so I'll talk to you later," I said, rushing him out.

"Are you ok?" he asked.

"Why wouldn't I be?"

"I know me and you tried to make us work."

"Oh, I'm not worried about it. I'm happy for you," I said, lying through my teeth.

"Aight, well I'mma head out," he said, kissing the babies. As I watched him walk out the door, I felt the tears building up in my eyes and in my heart. I felt like a complete idiot and if he would've come in at the same time as Jas, I would have felt like an even bigger idiot, pouring my heart out to a nigga already engaged to be married. If he proposed to her then I know he's in love with her. For some reason, no matter what problems we've had, I've always had it in my mind that he was my soulmate, the person made for me, but obviously I wasn't made for him. I was no longer gonna stress myself out and hold myself back from love. After getting the twins and Jasmine situated, I laid in my bed, stuck in my thoughts. When my phone started to ring, I quickly answered, after looking at the caller ID.

"Oh my God, you aren't gonna believe this shit!" I said as soon as I answered.

"I already know boo, how you holding up?" Camille asked.

"It feels like I'm in a fucking bad dream, but how did you already know?"

"He brought her bowling tonight and she called herself his fiancé. Bitch, I could've smacked the taste out her mouth."

"Why didn't you call me?"

"He begged me to wait. I figured he at least deserved to be the one who told you first."

"I guess. I was about to tell him how I felt. If Jasmine hadn't run in before him and spilled the beans, I would've embarrassed the shit out of myself," I said.

"Damn boo, I'm sorry. I didn't think about that."

"It's cool, but I have the biggest fucking headache, so I'mma call you tomorrow."

"I love you boo, and everything gonna be alright," Camille reassured me. Instead of replying to her, I just hung up the phone. Curling up in my bed, I cried until sleep took over my body.

Chapter Eight (Jason)

"Damn, so you really told her?" Kaliah asked.

"Yeah, I wanted to be the first person to tell her."

"How'd she take it?" she asked. I really didn't fucking feel like talking bout Lil Mama right now, but it seemed like Kaliah had twenty-one questions for a nigga.

"She took it well. She told me congratulations and wished me the best," I said nonchalantly.

"'And you believed her?" Kaliah asked with a smirk.

"Why wouldn't I believe her?" I asked her, getting pissed.

"I'm just saying. Y'all have been through alot together, got two kids, and you tell her that you've just asked another woman to marry you, and she took it well? It just doesn't sound right to me."

"What the fuck? It seems like you're trying to find a fucking issue with everything!'" I snapped.

"No babe, and I'm sorry if it seems that way."

"Yeah aight," I said, shaking my head.

"So do you think your friends liked me?"

"What do you think?" I asked.

"Hell naw!" she screamed before laughing.

"My bad about them. They have a loyalty to Cherish that's like none other," I said honestly.

"I can understand that I guess."

"You handled yourself really well."

"Thanks."

"I was just thinking, I don't have family for you to meet, but why haven't I met your family?" I questioned.

"Simply because you've never asked. I didn't want to rush things and run you away," she said nervously.

"Is that the only reason?"

"Yup." "Aight, well call them. We're gonna go see them this weekend," I told her. I didn't know what was going on with her and why she was being so fucking secretive, but she rarely talked about her parents and where she came from, and I thought that was weird.

Saturday came fast as hell and as we drove to meet her parents, Kaliah was silent and she looked scared as hell. Shit, she was making me feel bad for her. As we rode through a nice little suburban town in Jersey, she pulled into the driveway of a nice size yellow house. It was one of those houses from the movies, flowers all around it with a white picket fence. When she parked the car, I waited for her to get out the car, but she didn't. When I went to grab her hand to reassure her that everything was ok, I noticed she was shaking hard.

"Man, we ain't got to do this," I said, feeling like shit.

"No, I want to. I just pray you still love me after," she said sadly. Getting out the car, she walked up to the door of her parents' house and rang the doorbell.

"Kaliah!" a beautiful older woman screamed before pulling her in quickly and slamming the door in my face. Trying to keep my composure, I knocked on the door and waited for someone to answer it.

"I'm so sorry babe," Kaliah said when she answered."Don't worry about it," I said, walking into the house.

"This is my mother Katherine and this is my father, Keith," she said with a slight smile.

"It's nice to meet you both," I said politely.

"So you the one marrying my baby," he said, before firmly shaking my hand.

"Yeah, I am!" I said proudly.

"Not without my ok you're not."

"I mean, it is already done," I snapped.

"Hey daddy, ummm Mommy said you'd been working on a new project," Kaliah interrupted before shit could escalate.

"Yeah, you want to see?"

"I do," she said, pulling his arm, trying to take him out of the living room.

"Let go of me girl. Don't be rude, you didn't even ask Jason if he wanted to see some of my work."

"No daddy, I don't think he wants to," she said with pleading eyes.

"Let the man decide on his own."

"I don't mind," I shrugged. Following him down the hall and into a room, he told me to sit at a chair by his desk. I assumed this was his office. When I sat down, he handed me a photo album and when I opened it, I was shocked as hell.

"What is this?" I asked.

"I'm a photographer," he said with a smile.

"Are these real?" I asked.

"Now what kind of question is that?" he replied with a smirk. That's when I finally looked around his office and saw the pictures of Kaliah he had all over the walls. I saw pictures of Kaliah as a child, bound and gagged. As my eyes wandered onto a picture that literally made me sick to my stomach, all I could see was red as I grabbed him and beat the shit out of him.

"You fucking pervert, these are children!" I screamed, while continuing to pound him. All I could see was that naked picture of my daughter, propped up on some fucking bed.

"What the hell is wrong with you, get off my husband!" Kaliah's mother screamed as I continued to

pound on her perverted husband.

"You know what he does? You know what he did to your child and you just allowed it!" I screamed.

"It's just pictures. He ain't never touched her or any other child!" she tried to argue.

"It ain't just fucking pictures, this shit is illegal and fucking disgusting!"

"What's going on?"

"This nigga got a naked picture of Jasmine, my fucking daughter on his wall!"

"Oh my God!" Kaliah said, covering her mouth.

"I want y'all out my house before I call the police!" her father screamed.

"Oh yeah, please call the police!"

"Let's just leave," Kaliah said, grabbing my arm.

"If you knew what the fuck was going on, why would you still come here?" I said, pulling away.

"I just needed closure. He took those pictures of me for so long, I grew up thinking that they were normal." "You're a grown ass woman. I understand you as a child thinking it was normal, but as an adult, you had to have figured out that this shit wasn't right!" I snapped as we walked to the car. When we got inside the car, I wasted no time calling the police and reporting that nigga, while Kaliah listened with tears in her eyes. It took everything in my body not to kill that nigga and burn all those fucking pictures, but I had children to take care of and I damn sure wasn't trying to do that from a jail cell. When we got home, I didn't know what to say to Kaliah or how to feel. I guess the saying is true *most people don't look like what they've been through.* I never would have thought that she had parents that crazy. Now it made sense why she never really talked about them.

"I'm so sorry about your daughter. I hadn't been at that house since I was seventeen."

"It's fine Kaliah. I'mma handle the nigga that took them pictures!" I snapped, banging on the steering wheel.

"You know, when I went there, I had this plan. I was going to tell my parents that what my father did and what my mom allowed him to do wasn't normal. I wanted to stand up for myself, show them that even though they tried to fuck me up, I came out swinging and I did good by myself. But when I got there and I saw him, I felt like a child all over again. I felt scared, lost and confused. Everything I came there to say got caught in my throat and I just wanted to run away like I did so many years ago," she said while crying.

"You can talk to me. I you would have told me what happened, I wouldn't have pushed you to go see ya parents," I said, shaking my head.

"I'm so used to handling things on my own."

"Well you don't have to do that anymore, you have me," I said.

"I know that now babe, and I'm sorry for keeping you in the dark," she said. When we got in the house, she talked and I listened, she cried and I comforted her and dried her tears. I wasn't in love with Kaliah, but after tonight, I knew for certain that I loved her and had strong feelings for her.

Chapter Nine (Cherish)

I know that I'm the one to blame for losing you,

I really, really wish that I could be happy for you

There's just one thing I need you to do

Don't you touch her like you used to touch me

Don't you love her like you really needed me

Don't you love her like you used to love me

Baby, what hurts the most is letting go

I just want you to know that I love you so

I know things are different now

You've gone and settled down

    I thought for sure you'd always wait meI've been laying in the same spot since finding out that Mega was getting married, replaying the same song on my iPad. I literally feel like my heart has been ripped out of my body. I feel broken and lost. It's crazy how you replay an event over and over in your head and when it finally happens, it's totally different from what you imagined it to be. I expected me to tell Jason how I felt and for him to let me know that he felt the same way, and boom, we live happily ever after. I couldn't stop the overflow of tears from falling from my eyes, I'd just lost the only man I've ever loved.

I couldn't have prepared myself for the pain I was feeling right now.

"Cherish!" I heard someone scream. I wasn't sure who it was, but I was a fucking mess and I prayed that it wasn't Mega. As I laid in bed, I saw my bedroom door open and sighed in relief when I saw who it was.

"Look bitch, I know you're hurting right now, but it has been days!"

"How you even get in here?" I asked, rolling my eyes.

"What, you forgot you gave me a key?" she asked with a smirk.

"Girl, I gave it to you for emergencies, and this ain't an emergency."

"This is a fucking emergency. This is like Deja vu, but you wanna know the difference?" she asked."Not really, but I'm sure you're gonna tell me," I said smartly.

"Oh bitch don't get smart, but hell yeah I'mma tell you. What's different is instead of one child, you have three little fucking kids depending on you. So the fuck what he proposed to that home wrecking bitch, it's his loss!" she snapped.

"You don't understand Camille because you're in love, married and happy!" I snapped back.

"Girl bye. That damn nigga that makes me so happy ain't always make me happy. He broke my heart time and time again, but I didn't let it break me because I know my worth!"

"I just can't help but feel stupid as hell for even thinking that we could be happy together."

"That ain't stupid. Shit if you stupid, then so am I, so is Shante and so is every other bitch on the planet," she said laughing.

"Uh huh bitch, speak for yourself. I ain't stupid, I'm just in love," Shante said, walking into my bedroom.

"Whatever bitch," Camille said, rolling her eyes at Shante.

"Ain't nothing wrong with being in love and wanting it to work Cherish. Hell, I saw the bitch, so trust me when I say he might love that hoe, but he ain't in love," she said, rolling her eyes while going through my closet.

"How you know he ain't in love with her?" I asked.

"I can tell, us women know these things," she said nonchalantly.

"Whatever," I said with a wave of my hand. I mean why would he propose to a chick he ain't in love with.

"Ooooo, you got some nice clothes, make me wish I was a size ten for a minute," Shante said laughing.

"Seriously Cherish, you gotta get it together. You're too good of a person to be in so much pain. Fuck that nigga if he can't see it," Camille said.

"Hell yeah and if I were you, I'd invite that white boy on the trip," Shante said.

"Girl, don't listen to her. This is coming from the bitch that was chilling with Mark's cousin, knowing damn well Kasan hated that nigga. Don't be petty like her."

"Oh you tried it. I didn't know they didn't fuck with each other until it was too late. Shit, you gotta admit his rough ass was fine as hell," she said laughing.

" I'mma tell Kasan on ya ass," I said with a laugh.

"Kasan know he bae," she said with a shrug. "I think I will invite Peter. I mean, since all y'all broke the rules and y'all bringing y'all dudes, I might as well," I said. Grabbing my phone, I called Peter and waited for him to answer.

"Hey gorgeous," he said sweetly.

"Hey, I know this is kind of last minute being that we leave tomorrow, so if you can't make it I understand," I said quickly.

"Can you tell me what you're talking about before you go telling me that I can't make it," he said with a laugh.

"Yeah sorry, I just wanted to know if you would come with me to the Bahamas," I said nervously.

"I would love to come," he said.

"Oh wow, ok, I'll text you the info," I said with a big smile.

"Alright, see you tomorrow," he said before hanging up. After hanging up with him, I was feeling a lot better. I mean don't get me wrong, I was still hurt, but I finally felt like I could get over it. I thought the girls were gonna leave, but instead, they decided to stay the night with me and we would all leave for the airport together. Having friends that genuinely cared about me made my heart smile. It made me feel even better being able to talk to women who actually understood where I was coming from. We spent most of the night talking and drinking, and when we finally tapped out, we were all stretched out on my bed, talk about slumber party.

The next morning came way too fast and me and the girls were hungover and tired. While I finished packing, there was a knock at the door. Rushing to open the door for who I assumed was Mark, I swung it open, only to be face to face with Mega and Peter.

"Ummmmm, come in," I said, confused. I was expecting Peter to come, but I wasn't too sure why Jason was here.

"It's nice to meet you, I'm Peter," he said, before extending his hand for Mega to shake.

"What up, I'm Jason," he said, while shaking his hand.

"What are you doing here?" I asked Jason.

"I just came to bring you the suitcase you asked for the other day. I was hoping I caught you before you left."

"Damn, I forgot I asked you for that. Thank you because the one I have is just too small," I said with a laugh.

"You want me to go transfer your things to this suitcase?" Peter asked.

"Please, that would be awesome," I said kissing his cheek. When he walked into the other room, Mega's ass wasted no time with his jokes.

"I see you went on the vanilla side," Mega whispered to me with a smirk.

"You play so much," I said, rolling my eyes with a smirk.

"I'm just saying, I didn't know you did the white chocolate," he said with a shrug.

"I don't care what color they are as long as they treat me the way I deserve," I said honestly. As Mega stared into my eyes, I couldn't tell if the look on his face was jealously, or something else.

"And does he?"

"Does he what?"

"Treat you the way you deserve?"

"Yeah, he treats me good, but I'm taking it slow. Not everyone can just hop into a new relationship," I said smartly.

"I feel you, but I'mma let you finish getting ready. Have fun, be safe and call when you can," he said before walking out. When I was done packing, I hopped into the car, while Peter put my luggage into the trunk. Peter and I drove in front, while Shante and Camille drove behind us. Pulling up to the airport, we parked our cars and went to meet up with everyone else. As we got closer and closer to boarding, I got more and more nervous. I had never been out of Jersey, let alone on a plane and out of the country. All I could think about was shit like *Final Destination*, and that movie where Denzel's fine ass played a drunk pilot.

"You alright?" Peter asked, rubbing my back.

"Yeah, I'm fine," I lied.

"Girl, you look like you about to throw up," Shante said laughing.

"I'm just nervous as hell," I said with a smile. We waited a few minutes before everyone was there.

"Who's this?" Kasan asked, looking at Peter.

"This is my friend Peter. Peter, this is Shante's boyfriend, Kasan," I said, introducing them.

"What up?" Kasan said, attempting to dap him, only to have Peter reach his hand out to shake Kasan's.

"I ain't know you liked white boys," Chris said loudly.

"Don't be rude!" Queesha said, slapping his arm. Embarrassed to the highest power, I was now excited to be boarding the plane.

"I'm so sorry Peter," I said.

"It's fine, your friends are a bit rough around the edges though," he said with a laugh.

"Yeah, they are, but I love them," I said with a laugh.

Chapter Ten (Mega)

"So did you take her the luggage?" Kaliah asked.

"Yeah," I said.

"Was it just her and Camille that went?" she asked.

"Naw, everyone went, like a couple's trip."

"Oh, ok. I wonder why she didn't invite us," she replied nonchalantly. I was so confused by what the fuck she said, I didn't even respond. Why the fuck would Cherish invite me and my new fiancé on a trip?

"I'm just saying, I don't like being outcasted. They are your friends, just as much as hers."

"Kaliah, the trip is for her birthday. Do you think she likes you enough to invite you?" I said.

"She said we were cool."

"No, she said she was over the situation. Would you invite some chick on a trip that was dating your ex?" "I guess not, but I want to be able to do fun things with your friends like she does."

"Aight Kaliah," I said, before getting up and walking out the room. It was now getting to the point where she was obsessed with getting in good with everyone. I needed her to understand that it wouldn't be easy because they are friends with

Cherish, and at the end of the day, their loyalty lies with her. Walking upstairs, I went to check on the twins. It still amazed me how much they looked like me and I could also see so many traits of Lil Mama.

"Hey daddy, is Mama Ashley coming to see me today?" Jasmine asked.

"Naw baby, I don't think so."

"Maybe she doesn't want to see me anymore."

"Don't think that way, she loves you, something must have come up."

"Ok, but can you call her for me?"

"Aight," I said. When she walked out, I grabbed my phone and called Ashley, only for her not to answer. Getting the kids dressed and ready, I loaded them into the car and prepared to head out. After dropping them off at Cherish's house with the nanny, I headed straight to Ashley's apartment.

"Who is it?" I heard her say through the door after I knocked. "It's Mega, open the door."

"Can you come back later?"

"Yo, open this fucking door. You were so excited about reconnecting with Jas, only for you not to see her for weeks!" I snapped.

"I've been sick, but please don't take her from me."

"Open the door Ashley!" I snapped again. I could hear her unlock the door and what I saw shocked me.

"Come in," she said nervously.

"Is that nigga here?" I asked, reaching for my gun.

"No, she isn't here," she said, moving to the side.

"What happened to your face?" I asked, sitting on the couch.

"Me and Jayda got into a fight," she said lowly.

"Repeat that shit!"

"We got into a fight Mega, damn!"

"So you lettin that nigga put his hands on you?" I asked in disbelief.

"Friends fight and argue Jason. Don't be making it more than what it is."

"Fuck that, Ash. That bitch used to be a grown ass nigga. I don't give a fuck if that nigga got boobs, a pussy and a feminine voice, he still a nigga under all that!"

"Look, can you just tell Jas that I'm sick and I will see her soon."

"Yeah, I'll let her know. I'm telling you now, as long as you still got this nigga in ya life, you'll never get to be a mother to Jas. I won't allow her to see this bullshit!" I snapped, before getting up to leave.

"I know it was fucked up for me to do the shit I did, I just want you to know that I'm sorry. Now all I want is to be a part of my daughter's life."

"Actions speak louder than words. I remember you being the sassy girl that had a mind of her own and didn't give a fuck about what people had to say about her, and you damn sure didn't do shit you didn't want to do," I said, shaking my head.

"Well, that's the girl I'm trying to find again."

"I hope so, but let me head back home," I said, before walking out the door. Sitting in my car, all I could think about was the bruises on her face. I don't give a fuck how I feel about her, she's still my daughter's mother regardless. As I sat in my car, contemplating whether or not I should leave, my answer fell right in my fucking lap. I watched as Jayden came out the house, with Ashley close behind.

"I didn't tell him anything!"

"I don't give a fuck, why you let him in our apartment?"

"What was I supposed to do?"

"Tell that nigga to leave!"

"Why you being like this? I didn't do anything wrong, you heard the whole conversation!" Ashley pleaded. I didn't know what to think as they made a fool out of themselves, right outside their apartment. What I was watching didn't look like two friends arguing, it looked like they were in a full blown fucking relationship. As I continued to watch them argue, I watched as that nigga/bitch Jayden took things to the next level, by slapping the shit out of Ashley. Hopping out my car, I ran up to them and punched that nigga Jayden so hard, I heard his jaw crack.

"Jason, why the fuck would you do that!" Ashley snapped at me, while still on the ground from the slap this nigga landed across her face.

"Fuck you mean why I do that? You just gonna let this bitch beat on you!" I screamed in disbelief.

"She was just upset that I let you into our apartment," she explained, while trying to help him off the ground.

"Yo, stop saying she. This is a nigga who once had a dick between his leg!"

"Fuck you Mega!" Jayden screamed.

"Yeah, that's exactly what you want, but I wouldn't fuck you with the next nigga's dick, bitch!" I said with a smirk.

"I ain't did shit but try and love you, but now that love is gone!"

"I don't give a fuck about that shit. Ashley, come home with me and I'll help you," I said.

"Nigga, she ain't going with you because she's in love with me. She don't care how many times I beat her ass, she ain't never leaving me," he said laughing. Looking into Ashley's eyes, I could see her embarrassment, but I could also see that everything this nigga said was true. Giving her one last look, I turned around and walked away. I didn't have time to be dealing with her bullshit with that crazy nigga. If she wanted to stay with that he/she and continue to get her ass beat, that was her business. Pulling up to my house, I watched as Kaliah peeked through the window. I knew she was probably worried because I'd been gone longer than I expected. Walking up to my door, I used my key and unlocked it. When I walked into my house, I looked at the window that I saw her looking through, but Kaliah was nowhere to be found. Walking upstairs, I found her in bed reading a book. It was shit like this that made me feel like she wasn't built for a nigga like me. If you worried about a nigga, then say that, ain't no need to hide it and act like you don't care.

"What's up?" I asked. Walking into the bedroom, I started to undress, but from the corner of my eyes, I could see her watching my every move.

"Nothing, been reading, and did a little cleaning. Oh, and your dinner is in the oven," she said nonchalantly.

"Thanks babe," I said, before walking into the bathroom to take a shower. If she wasn't gonna ask me what happened or where I had been, then I ain't gonna tell her. I didn't have time to play these fucking games with her, I had too much on my mind. After showering and throwing on some basketball shorts and a wife beater, I went downstairs to take my food out the oven. I knew she didn't cook, but each and every time I opened the oven, I said a silent prayer in hopes that it was some real food. A nigga was again let down as I pulled the oven door open, only to be met with some chinese food. As I sat at the table eating, Kaliah walked into the kitchen and sat in the chair directly across from me.

"What's up?" I asked.

"How was your day?"

"It was straight."

"Oh ok, everything alright?" she asked nervously.

"Yeah, everything good. I went by Ashley's crib and some shit popped off with me and that bitch Jayden."

"What happened?"

"Man, that nigga beating on her. I told her to come home with me, but she didn't want to," I explained.

"You told her to come here?" she said, looking mad as hell.

"Yeah, I did. I know the way I punched that nigga he was gonna be mad as hell and take that shit out on her."

"You hit him?"

"That nigga slapped her hard as hell."

"I understand, but she's grown and we're dealing with enough shit from them, so why involve yourself?"

"That's my daughter's mom, regardless of the fucked up shit she's done. I ain't gonna let no one cause harm to the people I care about."

"Oh... I see," she said before getting up and walking out. I didn't know what her problem was or what she expected me to say, but obviously I didn't tell her what she wanted to hear.

Chapter Eleven (Cherish)

"Welcome to Ocean Club Resorts!" a beautiful woman greeted us.

"Thank you!" we all said at once. As I looked at my surroundings, it was breathtaking and I was excited. I had never been out of Jersey, so to be here in the Bahamas was huge for me.

"Yo, this shit nice as hell!" Chris said.

"Hell yeah, I'm tryna swim with some fish!" Camille said excitedly.

"Fuck that, I'm tryna see what they smoke be like out here," Kasan said seriously.

"Well, I've been here quite a few times. I could show you guys around, do a few activities," Peter said.

"Thanks," I said, kissing his cheek.

"So you know where they got that good good at?" Kasan asked.

"That good good?" Peter said, confused.

"Yeah, that smoke."

"What smoke? They do have an awesome party at night, with a bonfire and performances," he said, causing us all to laugh. I felt a little bad because he laughed right along with us, not knowing that the joke was on him.

"Naw, that kush, trees, reefer, weed…"

"Oh no, I will not assist in helping you obtain drugs," he responded, sounding appalled.

"Next time, we need to come alone," Peter whispered. Ignoring him, I just followed behind the man who would be showing us to our rooms. I made sure to book a room with two bedrooms, just in case things didn't physically work out between me and Peter. I was glad that I did because he was working my nerves. I never noticed how bougie he was, even after spending so much time with him, but it definitely showed when he came around my friends.

"This is your room," I said when we walked into our room.

"My room?"

"Yeah… Is that a problem?"

"No, I just assumed we would share the same room," he said with a disappointed face.

"You know I'm trying to take things slow. I thought us sharing a room would be rushing things a bit."

"That's fine," he said, before taking his luggage to the bedroom. Walking into my bedroom, I walked out on my balcony and was taken aback at how beautiful the view was. The water was crisp and blue. It damn sure didn't look like any water I'd ever seen. As I took in the view, I was interrupted by my ringing phone.

"Hey boo," I answered.

"Girl, this shit is so beautiful!" Camille screamed into the phone.

"I know right, I was just looking at the water."

"You wanna go to the beach?" she asked.

"Hell yeah, I'mma hop in the shower and then I'll be down."

"Aight, and see if Peter wants to come," she said, before hanging up. Walking into Peter's room, I noticed that he was already unpacked and about to hit the shower. As I stared at his body, I couldn't help but notice his imprint in the towel. I guess the saying wasn't true that white boys weren't packing, because from the looks of it, he was packing something heavy.

"Everything ok?" he asked. Snapping me out of my thoughts, I slowly nodded my head, but didn't once take my eyes off his body.

"Well are you gonna say something?" he asked with a smirk.

"Uhhhhh yeah, we're all going to the beach, do you want to go?"

"Yes, I would love to go for a swim in something warm," he said, licking his lips.

"Oh well...ok just...ummm yeah... I'mma... yeah I'mma go," I said, tongue tied like a muthafucka. Backing out of the room while still staring at him, I didn't notice his empty suitcase. As if I wasn't already embarrassed enough, I tripped over the suitcase and fell ass first onto the floor.

"Are you ok?" he asked as he reached to help me up, but before he could, he tripped and fell right along with me. As we both laid on the floor, we were cracking up laughing at how nervous and crazy we were acting, as if we didn't know each other.

"I'mma go get washed and dressed, I'll see you in a little bit," I said, once I was up. I wasted no time making a run for it. Opening my suitcase, I searched for the perfect outfit to wear with my bathing suit. I decided that I would be extra sexy this whole trip. I mean, a girl only turns eighteen once, so why not go all out? Pulling out my bikini and a pair of short jean shorts, I placed them on the bed. Walking into the bathroom, I ran a bath and was very excited to see the Jacuzzi tub that was calling my name. After spending almost an hour in the tub, I got out and wrapped a fluffy oversized towel around my body. When I was dressed and ready to go, I walked out of my room, only to find Peter waiting for me outside of my door.

"Wow!" he said when he saw me.

"Is that a good wow?" I asked sexily.

"Hell yeah it is!"

"Thank you," I said, blushing.

"No thank you, are you ready to go?"

"Yeah, I'm ready," I said. Throwing my hair into a ponytail and adding some lip gloss, my look was complete and I was ready to go. When we got downstairs, everyone was already there, except the person who planned it. I'm almost certain that Camille and Mark were somewhere being nasty, I could bet my life on that.

"So we just waiting for Camille and Mark?" I asked, shaking my head.

"Yeah, you know that bitch is always late, but stop tryna take the focus off ya sexy ass," Shante said.

"I don't know what you talkin bout," I said with a laugh.

"Uh huh girl, I see you working with a little stuffy back there," Shante said, looking at my ass.

"Yassssss bitch, where that ass come from?" Shana said.

"Come here babe, look at this shit," Queesha said to Chris. Ignoring her, he shook his head and walked away.

"You so fucking messy," Shana said to Queesha.

"What I do?" she asked.

"You know if he would have looked at her ass you would have smacked the life out his ass!" Shana said laughing.

"Bye bish, I don't know about you, but I gotta keep Chris' ass on his toes," she shrugged.

"Y'all a mess, but yeah, the twins did a bitch body right," I said through laughter. As we talked and laughed, we were having so much fun in the lobby, we decided to wait ten more minutes, before heading to the beach without them. When we got there, it was beautiful. From the sand, to the water and trees. As we played in the water, while the men sat on the beach smoking with some locals who worked there, I glanced over at Peter. He was sitting off to the side and the look on his face let me know that he didn't approve of what the other men were doing. I couldn't help but think of how much fun I would be having if Mega was here. Don't get me wrong, Peter was fun to be around and he always made sure I was taken care of, but the fact still remained that he didn't fit in with my friends.

"Girl, you see ya man!" Shante said laughing.

"Yeah girl, he looks like he's having the worst time," Queesha said laughing.

"I know. I guess he doesn't really want to be around them."

"I can understand that. I mean he came for you, to spend time with you," Shana said.

"Yeah, I know, but I just wanted him to get to know the men in my life."

"Hey boo's!" Camille said when she finally showed up.

"Don't hey boo us bitch. How you gonna set some shit up and don't show up!" I playfully snapped as she moved closer to us in the water.

"My bad, this island air got me feeling real horny," she said seriously.

"Uh huh bitch, you nasty!" I said.

"Whatever bitch, if you were nasty with that boy, maybe he wouldn't be sitting over there angry right now."

"We said the same thing. He looking like he don't wanna be here," Shante said. Looking over at him, I felt bad, so I walked out of the water and went to check on him.

"You ok?" I whispered.

"No, this smell is getting on my nerves. I don't understand how people like them can put that nasty stuff in their systems."

"People like them?" I asked, offended.

"Druggies."

"Druggies?"

"Yes, that is drugs they're doing, and it's illegal."

"Ok Peter, well I would have never invited you on this trip if I knew you would be a Debbie downer," I said before walking away.

Chapter Twelve (Ashley)

"Are you ok?"

"Shut the fuck up talking to me!" Jayda snapped at me.

"What did I do wrong?" I asked, while we sat in the hospital, waiting to be seen.

"It's your fault he fucking hit me!"

"He wouldn't have hit you if you didn't hit me."

"You shouldn't have had him in our crib, damn!"

"You shouldn't have been fucking with him and Cherish!" I snapped.

"Oh, so now you taking this bitch side?"

"I'm just saying Jayda. None of this would have happened if you didn't keep fucking with that man."

"I loved him," she said with teary eyes.

"You deserve to be with someone who loves you, just as such as you love them."

"And let me guess, you're that person, right?" she said with a smirk.

"No, I don't think I am," I said honestly.

"Oh, so you don't love me anymore Ashley?"

"I love you Jayda, but not enough to continue to deal with this shit."

"This nigga Jason got you singing a new tune," she said laughing.

"You don't love me, you don't do women, remember? So why are you even acting like you care about whether or not I still want to be with you."

"I don't... but I don't appreciate you jumping ship," she said, jumping up right in the middle of the hospital.

"I ain't jumping ship because of Mega. Look at how you treat me Jayda. Here I am at the hospital for ya ass and you look like you about to hit me, I can't do this!" I snapped. Grabbing my purse, I got up and prepared to walk away. As soon as I turned to leave, I was yanked back by my hair. I couldn't catch my balance and hit the floor hard.

"Bitch, you think you can just leave me!" she screamed, while raining painful blows on my body as I screamed for her to stop. Before I knew what was happening, Jayda was being pulled off me and being dragged away in handcuffs.

"I'mma kill you bitch!" she screamed.

"Are you ok?" a police officer asked me.

"I'm fine, thank you," I said, while rubbing my face.

"You don't look fine and I really think you should get checked out."

"No, I just want to get out of here," I said, turning to walk away. Before I could take a step, everything went black and I passed out. When I woke up, I was hooked up to an IV and on the side of me was the officer who had helped me out.

"How long was I out?" I asked.

"A few hours. The doctor gave you something for the pain, you have a concussion," he said sympathetically.

"Thank you, can I leave now?"

"Listen, I don't know your situation and I won't pretend that I do, but it isn't healthy for you to allow that woman to abuse you the way she just did."

"I know, and I'm done with her. I'm so tired of giving everything I have to someone who doesn't deserve it." "How long have you guys been together?" he asked.

"We have never been together, she's just my friend."

"Hmmp ok. Well do you have somewhere to go?"

"I might, do you have my purse?" I asked. When he handed it to me, I pulled out my phone and called Mega, but he didn't answer. Hanging up, I couldn't help the tears that left my eyes. Since I could remember, everything in my life had been so hard. Now here I was, an ex drug addict, a hoe and a stripper, with an abusive girlfriend that used to be a man and a daughter who barely knows me anymore.

"Hey, hey, please don't cry. If your friend didn't answer that's fine, you can stay with me," he said. Looking up, I noticed that he wasn't the most handsome man. Standing at 5'6, he was a little on the heavy side and looked to be about forty years old, black as tar, with the brightest teeth I'd ever seen. But to be honest, he was the nicest man I'd met since Jason and for that, he was the sexiest man on earth right now.

"I don't want to impose, I have enough money for a motel."

"You're not imposing. I didn't handle your case because I was off duty, so it isn't even a conflict of interest. I think you're beautiful and in need of a friend and I want to help," he said sweetly and sincerely.

"Thank you," I said with a smile. On the drive to his house, I told him all about Jayda and when I was finished, he drove with his mouth hung open. I mean shit, from the outside looking in, Jayda was a beautiful woman, so I knew he would be surprised to find out that she was once a man.

"Honestly, I didn't know. I mean in my line of work I deal with all types of domestic disputes, so I just assumed she was a crazy girlfriend."

"Yeah, well I'm done with her and I just want to focus on becoming a better mom and woman," I said honestly.

"As long as you mean it, I have no problem helping you achieve it," he said with a smile.

"I'm sorry I was so worried about myself, I didn't even ask you about you."

"Well my name is Tyler and I'm forty-two. I don't have any children and my wife recently passed tonight from AIDS"

"Wow, I'm sorry for your loss," I said sincerely. I couldn't help but wonder if he was sick also. He didn't look like he was, but you never know.

"I know what you're thinking and no I don't have the virus. My wife had been battling with a drug addiction for some time and we were separated for years. I tried to help her as much as I could, but it wasn't enough. A few months ago, she had finally decided to get clean, but by then, it was too late, she already had full blown AIDS."

"That's so sad. I battled and still continue to battle with drug addiction, so I know how hard it is."

"Yeah, she's battled with the disease for years, but she got clean and we were happy for a while. She got pregnant and our daughter died from SIDS. That was too much for her to bare and she just went over the edge," he said as he pulled up to a beautiful house. When he parked, I followed behind him into his home and was taken aback by how beautiful and homey the inside was.

"Do you have anything I can wear, I really want to shower," I said. Walking into his bedroom, he opened a drawer and handed me an oversized t-shirt and a pair of basketball shorts.

"I have to go to work, I won't be back until 5am, so you can have the bed. I usually take the couch anyways."

"Thank you so much for everything, you don't even know me."

"I know enough, and I like what I know," he said, before walking back out the door. Sitting on the edge of the tub and turning on the water, I couldn't help but think that maybe this was my happy ending.

Chapter Thirteen (Mega)

Waking up from the longest nap I'd ever taken, I popped up and looked at my clock. I couldn't believe that a whole day had gone by without as much as a text message. Grabbing my phone, as soon as I unlocked it, I noticed that I had over fifty text messages and a hundred missed calls. I also realized that my phone was set to silent.

"Kaliah!" I screamed. When she walked into the room, she had the biggest smile on her face that I wanted to slap off.

"How did you sleep?" she asked.

"Did you turn my fucking ringer off!"

"Why are you cursing at me nigga? Yeah, I turned it off, you were tired and it was ringing like a fucking party line!" she snapped.

"I'm a fucking father, what if something was wrong with the kids? I'm a businessman, so what if it was about one of my artist!"

"I didn't think about that. I just knew how peaceful you looked sleeping."

"Don't touch my phone man, damn!"

"Alright!"

"I'm serious, Kaliah. Don't touch my fucking phone again, that shit wasn't cool!"

"I heard you the first time, Jason!" she said, before storming away. Looking through my phone, I saw that it was a lot of calls and text messages from Ashley, and because of the shit that went down, I decided to call her first. After dialing her number, I waited for her to answer and when she didn't, I just hung up. Listening to my voice messages, one said that she was at the hospital with a concussion, and she was leaving Jayda and needed somewhere to stay. The next said that she was ok and would be staying with a friend for a while. After checking my voicemail, I called the kids and checked on them. Once I was sure that they were fine, I got dressed and headed to check on Mama Betty. Kasan had given me her spare key before he left and I swore to that nigga that I would check on her. Plus, I needed to get out of this house, I couldn't believe that she had touched my phone. Usually when I needed to get away, I went to see Mark and them. Shit was weird as hell not having my crew around. They were in the Bahamas, while I was in the states, wishing a nigga was on vacation.

"You leaving?" she asked.

"Yeah why, what's up?"

"Nothing, just asking," she said. Without another word, I walked out the door and into my car. When I pulled up to Mama Betty's house, I noticed that all the lights were off. Using my key, I unlocked the door and walked in. Looking around the house, I couldn't see any signs that Mama Betty was there and I got worried, so I headed to her bedroom. Opening the door, I was hit with a sight that could have blinded me. Mama Betty was bent over the bed, getting her back blown out by some nigga I couldn't see.

"What the fuck Mama Betty!" I snapped. Jumping up, she quickly grabbed the blanket and wrapped it around her body.

"Boy, you ain't ever heard of knocking. I oughta beat ya ass, how did you get in here!"

"Beat my ass? You in here being nasty with some nigga!"

"This ain't just some nigga, this my boyfriend," she said with a smile.

"How you doing son?" he said, reaching his hand out to shake mine.

"Nigga, put some clothes on and wash ya hands!" I snapped, as I stared at his hand as if it had the fucking package."Don't be talking to him like that. I'm grown and you ain't the man of this house. You betta take ya ass back to Cherish and be the man there!"

"You gotta go, so grab ya shit and start moving!" I snapped. I couldn't help but think about how Kasan would feel if he was here and saw his mama in this way.

"I'm so sorry, Leroy. Don't pay this boy no mind, he's my son's little friend. I'll call you," she said, before kissing him passionately. I didn't know whether to beat his fucking ass or go throw up. What sent me over the deep end was when he grabbed her ass.

"Fuck this shit!" I said, before yoking him up and tossing him out of her room. When he was gone, I went and sat at the kitchen table, while she went to go put some clothes on. When she came out, she slapped the shit out of me, but I already knew that was coming.

"Boy, what the hell is wrong with you?"

"Mama Betty, you too old to be doing this shit!"

"Boy, what shit!"

"Being a damn thot!" I screamed. Once again, she slapped the taste out my mouth.

"Never have I ever been a damn thot. Me and Leroy been together for months and I like him."

"Ain't no way Kasan gonna accept this!"

"Kasan ain't got no choice, he ain't going nowhere. What, you want me to be lonely?"

"You ain't lonely Mama Betty. You got Kasan, me and the kids."

"I ain't talking bout that kinda lonely, Jason. I need companionship, the kind I can only get from a man, not my damn son. Besides that, how many times have you come to see me this month, aside from dropping my babies off to see me," she said. When I thought about it, I realized that it had been weeks since I'd stopped by just to spend time with her.

"You're right and I'm sorry, I will do better."

"I don't need you to do better, because unlike you and my hard headed son, I understand that y'all have to have a life outside of me. I love Kasan, but he's grown. I did my job with him and now I need some love in my life. Shit, I ain't that old, I wanna get my groove on too," she said laughing. I felt uncomfortable talking to my boy's mama about her love life and shit. This was something she needed to talk to him about when he came home.

"Aight, that's enough. I understand and my bad for tripping." "Thank you baby, but you need to be apologizing to Leroy."

"Aight," I said.

"Well now that we got that worked out, I'mma need for you to get ghost. Leroy parked down the street, waiting for your crazy ass to leave," she said laughing.

"Aight, I'm out," I said, shaking my head.

"Oh, before you go, I'mma need that key," she said. I thought she was playing until I realized that she didn't crack a smile.

"Seriously, Kasan told me I gotta make sure you good."

"You damn straight. Next time, call before you come. I can take care of myself, tell him that," she said, before kissing my cheek. I felt like Tyrese on *Baby Boy*, I guess mama need a life too. Walking to my car, I pulled off, scarred for life. As I drove home, I couldn't help but feel a little hurt. This was some shit that only Cherish would understand and laugh at, but I couldn't call her because we didn't have that relationship anymore. Finally saying fuck it, I dialed her number and she answered on the first ring.

"Are my babies ok?" she asked.

"Yeah, they straight. I had some funny shit to tell you," I said, before telling her exactly what happened. "Oh shit you lying, Kasan gonna fucking go off," she said laughing.

"Man, this nigga had her bent over like she was a youngin."

"Shit, as we get older us women get riper, so I can believe it," she said, cracking up.

"Are you getting riper?" I asked.

"Boy bye, ask ya fiancé that," she said laughing.

"I'm just playing damn, but are you having fun?"

"Yeah, we about to go party right now, to bring my birthday in."

"Damn aight, I'll check you later, have fun," I said.

"I will," she replied before hanging up.

Chapter Fourteen (Cherish)

"Who was that on the phone?" Peter asked when I hung up, still laughing.

"Oh, that was Jason," I said nonchalantly.

"Well what's so funny, I would like to laugh too."

"Nothing, but I'm about to go to Camille's room, I'll be back."

"Alright, well I'll be ready to go by the time you make it back," he said, kissing my cheek. At midnight, I will be eighteen years old and I was bringing in my birthday turning up. Walking down the hall, I knocked on Shante's door first.

"What's up boo, I was just getting ready," she said when she answered.

"I gotta tell y'all something, so meet me in Camille's room," I said laughing. When I got to Camille's room, I could hear them arguing about something. Knocking on the door, I waited for one of them to answer. "Ummmm, should I come back?" I asked when Camille answered.

"Hell naw, this nigga just mad cuz I won't give his horny ass none of this good shit."

"Oh my God, y'all so nasty!" I said, walking into her room.

"No, he so nasty. He knows we about to go out and I'm already dressed," she said, shaking her head.

"Hey Mark," I said.

"Yeah yeah," he said, waving me off, all while having a mad face.

"He's such a spoiled brat. I tell him no one time in all the years we've been together and he acts like this," she said laughing. It wasn't long before Shante and the rest of the girls came knocking on the door. When they were all there, I told them what happened.

"So tell me why Jason went to check on Mama Betty and caught her fucking!"

"What, stop lying!" Camille screamed. I looked over at Shante and she just sat there with her hand over her mouth.

"Yo, Kasan is gonna flip. He swear his mama like the virgin Mary and shit," Shante finally said, laughing. "Yes bitch and when he caught her, she told his ass to give her the spare key and call next time," I said, cracking up.

"Oh my God, Mama Betty done got her groove back and shit!" Camille said.

"I been knew she was fucking, I'm just surprised that she got caught."

"Me too!" Camille cosigned.

"How y'all knew?"

"She was wearing makeup and shit, tryna get sexy for somebody," Shante said laughing.

"For real, that's what y'all do!" Mark said from the door.

"What, we ain't do shit," Camille said laughing.

"Y'all in here gossiping about my auntie."

"Boy bye, we talking!" Camille said, rolling her eyes.

"Anyways, y'all ready to go? I mean ya birthday is in an hour," Shante said.

"Yeah, I'm ready. I gotta go add some lip gloss and grab Peter, then we'll meet y'all downstairs," I said, getting up and preparing to walk out. When I got back to my room, Peter was ready and he actually seemed excited. Walking into the bathroom, I fixed my hair a little and added some lips gloss. Tonight I was wearing a tight, tan leather skirt with a split that stopped just before my coota, a white shirt that stopped just above my belly button and white wedges. Snapping a picture of myself, I added it to Facebook and Instagram. As soon as I added it, I started getting a bunch of likes. Since being single, I decided to start an Instagram page and as soon as I made it and posted a few pics, my follower number began to increase. I don't know most of them. A few of the men I know from around the way, but for the most part, my Instagram is full of strangers. Walking out of the bathroom, me and Peter walked out of the room, arm and arm, and when we got downstairs, all eyes were on me.

"Well damn, you really showing out, huh bitch!" Camille said, hugging me.

"I mean I only turn eighteen once, right?"

"You damn straight," she replied.

"Awwww, you look beautiful. I love this outfit on you!" Shante said.

"Thanks boo," I said with a smile. Walking out of the hotel, I searched for the car we had ordered, but I guess it was late because I only saw a damn limo.

"Come on girl!" Shana said, walking up to the limo. "Girl, that ain't ours, you can't do that," I said, scared.

"It's your birthday!" Camille screamed before running to the limo. When we were all in, our first stop was to some club. Pulling up, we gave our name and they let us straight through.

"Oh my God, it's so turnt in here!" I screamed.

"Hell yeah!" Queesha said laughing. We headed straight for the V.I.P and I wasn't sitting there five minutes, before some sexy ass dude with dreads asked me to dance. Standing up and grabbing his hand, he led me to the dance floor. As I danced with this stranger, he matched every sway and every grind, as if he knew my body. I loved a man that could dance, that shit did something to me and he was damn sure working my body. I was having so much fun and I was even happier when the girls joined me on the dance floor with men that didn't belong to them. I watched as Shante dominated the dance floor. She was so confident and I loved that about her. I could tell that it was rubbing off on me. After dancing to five songs, we were all tired and out of breath. Excusing ourselves, we walked to the V.I.P area.

"So, I wanna make a toast, so grab ya glass!" Camille said.

"Yeeeeeeeee!" Shante screamed. I guess the song that came on was her shit.

"I just wanna say happy birthday to my boo, my little sis and one of my best friends. You have been through so much and you handled it all like the G you are. I can't imagine not having you in my life and I'm so thankful that you allowed all of us to share this special day with you. Baby you've been grown for a long time, but now you're legally grown, so turn the fuck up!" she said with teary eyes.

"Awwww, thanks boo!" I said, hugging her.

"You are such a strong person and you deserve the world in my eyes," Camille said, causing me to tear up.

"Yeah, you do. When I first met you I thought, who is this damn girl trying to steal my bestie, but then I got to know you and to know you is to love you. You have become a little sister to us all and we love you boo!" Shante said, causing me to tear up.

"Yasssssss Lil Mama, we all love you, and through whatever, we will always have your back!" Shana said, hugging me.

"Awwwww, thanks y'all!" I said, hugging them. We were dancing in V.I.P, when my cellphone began to go off. After walking outside so I could hear, I answered the phone.

"Hello?"

"Happy birthday mommy!" I heard my baby Jas scream. "Thank you baby girl, what you doing up this late?"

"I waited until twelve so I could call you," she said, causing my heart to smile.

"Awwwww, I feel so loved," I said.

"Daddy wants to talk to you," she said.

"Hello?"

"Happy birthday Lil Mama," I heard Mega say sexily.

"Thank you, Jason."

"So are you having fun?" he asked.

"Yeah, we're at the club now."

"I saw them damn pictures you posted, when you start dressing like that?"

"When I turned eighteen," I said laughing.

"Yeah I bet, but you looking good."

"Thank you."

"I just wanted to tell you how proud I am. You are a great mother to Jasmine and the twins, and I see your growth, even if I don't say it."

"I'm glad you see it. I felt bad for the shit that went down at your house."

"I should've told you about me and Kaliah, but I didn't and for that I was wrong."

"Well, I gotta get back inside. Tell the kids I love them and give them kisses for me," I said before hanging up. Hearing that hoe's name just reminded me of the sad truth, he was going to marry her. She would soon be his wife and me just his baby mama. I hated that term, but let's be real, that's what I would be called. If you would have told me a year ago that I would have these babies and me and Jason would be separated, I would've called you crazy. I must have been on the phone too long because when I hung up, the girls were coming out of the club.

"Y'all ready to leave?" I asked.

"Hell naw, the men ready to head back to the hotel, so they about to come scoop us," Camille said. As we stood outside waiting, one of the men that we danced with walked up to Shante.

"Damn queen, you like Cinderella. You rushed off so fast, I didn't get ya number."

"I can't give you my number, sorry."

"Ok, can you just tell me where you will be at and I will make sure I'm there," he said. He was very handsome, with shoulder length dreads and some sexy ass lips.

"I don't know…" Just as she was about to answer, the limo pulled up with the guys. I was nudging Shante, but she wasn't paying me no mind, she was too busy giggling at the dude.

"What the fuck is so funny!" Kasan screamed out of the limo window. I watched as Shante's whole body stiffened, but she quickly loosened up.

"I gotta go," she said to the dude, before turning and getting into the limo.

"Tae baby, don't fucking play with me!"

"What are you talking bout Kasan?" she said nonchalantly.

"You really gonna make me fuck you up!" he snapped.

"Nigga, I wish you would. I'm sure y'all were doing way worse at the club y'all went to, so don't play with me!" Shante snapped.

"You always flipping and bouncing shit. We ain't talking bout me, we talking bout you standing in some nigga face!"

"Ok Kasan, like I said, I wasn't doing shit. He asked me for my number and that was it."

"Cut it out y'all!" Camille said, shaking her head at them.

"This nigga started it, acting all jealous and shit."

"Well it's Cherish's birthday, so cut it out."

"They're fine. I had an awesome birthday, now I just wanna go to sleep," I said laughing. As we drove in the limo back to the hotel, Shante and Kasan continued to argue back and forth. When the limo pulled up to the hotel, I was ready to fly out because I couldn't take one more minute of Camille and Mark making out next to me like I wasn't even there.

"Happy birthday baby," Peter said, when we made it back to the room.

"Thanks love," I said, hugging him.

"Did you have fun tonight?"

"Yeah, we danced and got wasted. What about you, did you have fun too?" I said laughing.

"No, it wasn't really my thing. I mean the whole popping bottles and smoking weed."

"Oh ok, well I'm sorry you didn't have a good time tonight."

"Well the night is still young and I have you with me," he said, grabbing my waist. Standing up on my tippy toes, I wrapped my arms around his neck and kissed him passionately. I wasn't sure if it was the liquor or my hormones, but I wanted him bad right now. Gripping my ass, he lifted me up and carried me to the bedroom. When we were there, he laid me gently on the bed. Climbing on top of me, he caressed my face and I suddenly felt uncomfortable. I felt like he was trying to make love to me and that was the last thing on my mind. I wanted to be fucked, nothing more nothing less. Jumping up from underneath him, I began taking my clothes off quickly. I watched as he removed his clothes and his body was so damn buff and sexy. My mouth was watering just wondering what the rest of him looked like.

"Are you sure you want to do this?" he asked sincerely.

"Peter, if I didn't want this, I would have let you know," I said, becoming frustrated. Don't get me wrong, I love how caring and attentive he is, but sometimes you just want to be taken without all that extra mess. There were times when I didn't even have to tell Mega anything. Shit, he didn't give me a chance to. He would just rip my clothes off and fuck me like it was the last piece he would ever get, that's what I needed right now.

"I wanna taste you," he said hungrily. Laying my naked body on the bed, I sat back and waited for him to devour my cookie with his lips, but all I felt was a nibble and then a series of dry licks, like a damn cat. Looking down at him, I couldn't figure out if he was playing or if he was serious. When he lifted his head, the look on his face told me that he was dead serious. Laying my head back down, I closed my eyes and tried to get myself into what he was doing, but it wasn't working. This shit right here was terrible. In my mind, it couldn't get any worse, but I guess I had spoken too soon because one minute he was licking my clit fast, and the next minute he had bit down on it.

"Ahhhhhhh!" I screamed, before punching him in the head.

"Owww, what the fuck Cherish!" he snapped at me.

"I'm soooo sorry. It was my reflexes, you bit me Peter!"

"You didn't like it?" he asked.

"No, it hurt, who would like that?"

"My ex-girlfriend loved it," he said smartly.

"Well, I didn't," I said. Not wanting to mess up the mood any more than what it was, I pushed him down on the bed and pulled his boxers off. I was starting to think that it just wasn't meant for us to have sex. I couldn't even see his actual dick, just a bunch of skin. It looked like his dick was playing peekaboo. I wasn't a sex pro, so I was clueless. I didn't know much, but one thing I knew was that I wasn't putting my mouth on that and he was damn sure using a condom, but that was gonna happen regardless.

"Do you have a condom?" I asked.

"Yeah, but before we take things further, I have to ask you something."

"Ok."

"Are we planning on being together after tonight?"

"Why can't we just enjoy each other? Why do we have to mess things up by adding a label?" I said, confused.

"I have feelings for you Cherish and I thought you had feelings for me too."

"I do and you know that. I love spending time with you," I said honestly.

"So what's stopping you?"

"I just feel like with Jason, we kinda rushed into things and that turned out horrible, so now I just want to take my time."

"I understand, but I'm not the friend kind of man. If I have sex with a woman, it's because she's my woman."

"So what are you saying?"

"I'm saying you're worth the wait and maybe we should just wait," he said, surprising me.

"I guess you're right, but can you at least stay in my room tonight?" I said, laying beside him and curling up.

Chapter Fifteen (Ashley)

I've been with Tyler for three days now and he is one of the nicest people I've ever met. He doesn't treat me like an object and he isn't nice to me because of what's between my legs, he is a genuinely kind hearted person.

"Hey, are you up?" I asked, when I walked into the living room. He had been sleeping on the couch since I'd been here and has been a complete gentleman.

"Yeah, what's up, you good?" he asked.

"I'm fine, how are you?" I asked.

"I'm ok. I got a good amount of sleep in."

"Well I wanted to tell you that I was going back to my apartment later on today."

"Now wait a minute Ashley, I don't know if it was something I did or said to make you want to leave, but please understand she will continue to abuse you."

"No, you didn't do anything, I just want to grab my things." "Is there something else you need me to buy?" he asked sweetly.

"Oh no, but my car is parked there, some pictures of my daughter and my important papers are there. I just want to grab that stuff."

"I understand, let me get dressed and I'll take you."

"Maybe I should just catch a cab. I don't know if she's there or not and I definitely don't want you to get dragged into my drama."

"I don't mind, I'm a cop, drama is my life," he said with a smile.

"Ok," I said. I was actually really scared to go back because I wasn't sure of what she would do if she was there.

"You ready?" he asked ten minutes later. When I looked up, he still had his work uniform on and I got nervous.

"You sure you wanna wear that?"

"What, you embarrassed to be seen with a cop? Don't worry, I don't have the car," he said with a laugh.

"No, I'm not embarrassed of you at all. I'm ready if you are," I replied with a smile. When we got into his car, it seemed like the longest ride ever. As he drove to my apartment, I said a silent prayer, hoping she wasn't there. When we pulled up to the apartment, he parked and we both got out of the car. Using my key, I unlocked the door and walked in with Tyler closely behind me. As soon as I made it close to my bedroom, I heard Jayda loud and clear, fucking in her bedroom. Ignoring the moans, I walked into my room and started stuffing stuff into my duffle bag.

"What the fuck you doing here!" I heard her scream behind me. When I turned around, she was naked and looked pissed off.

"I don't want any problems, I just came to get my stuff and I'm leaving."

"You don't leave until I say you can," she said with a calm voice.

"Why the fuck you worried about me when you were just in there fucking some nigga?"

"I hope you don't think you taking that car. What, you forgot it was in my name?" she said with a smirk.

"Is everything alright?" Tyler asked with his gun drawn.

"Yeah Tyler, everything is fine. I got what I need and I'm ready to go," I said, rolling my eyes.

"So you brought the fucking cops, really Ashley!" "He's a cop, but he's my friend, he ain't on duty!"

"So you fucking him?"

"I like him and he treats me the way I deserve, which is more than I can say for you!"

"You've been gone for a few days and all of a sudden you fucking with this old ass nigga!"

"I'm out!" I said, before walking past her, only for her to grab my arm.

"You better let her go. I ain't on duty and I know you a fucking nigga, so don't think I won't knock you the fuck out!" Tyler snapped. With a shocked face, Jayda looked at me with hurt in her eyes.

"You told him?" she said calmly.

"What he mean you a nigga!" her company said out of nowhere. I didn't know he had been listening and I kind of felt bad for telling Tyler. I wouldn't have said it if I'd known that he would go blasting it. Grabbing his arm, I pulled him into the living room and out the door, while Jayda and her company argued.

"I can't believe you said that!" I snapped on him when we got to the car.

"What the fuck, how you mad at me? That dude put his hands on you!" he snapped back.

"So what, I had the situation handled!"

"Oh, like you had it handled when we met?" he said, before pulling off. I didn't know how to respond because I knew he was right, so instead of replying, I sat back and enjoyed the silence.

"I wanted to make one more stop," I said before we could make it back to his house.

"Where do you need to go?"

"I wanna see my daughter," I said, putting the address into his GPS. Grabbing some makeup, I looked into the mirror, while retouching my face. I still had a couple bruises left over that I didn't want her to see. Pulling out my phone, I called Mega and made sure it was ok for me to stop by. I really missed my baby, so when he agreed, I was beyond thrilled. Pulling up to his house, I could tell that Tyler was in awe by how big Mega's house was.

"Your ex lives here?" he asked.

"Yeah, do you want to get out?"

"No, you go head and spend time with your baby. I'mma go get some rest and you can call me when you're ready to go," he said. Getting out the car, he came and opened my door like the gentleman he was, and walked me to the door. Ringing the doorbell, I waited for Mega to answer and when he did, he looked confused as hell. "Hey, thanks for letting me see her at such short notice," I said to Mega.

"No problem, is everything aight?" he said, while looking at Tyler.

"Oh, everything is good, this is my friend Tyler. Tyler, this is my daughter's father, Jason," I said, introducing them. Reaching his hand out, Tyler shook Mega's hand firmly. He didn't seem fazed or jealous, and that just made me more attracted to him.

"Nice to meet you. My bad if I scared you," he said with a laugh.

"Hell yeah, I ain't tryna see no police at my door," Mega said laughing with him.

"Aight beautiful, I'mma head out. Call me when you're ready and have fun," he said before kissing my hand and walking away.

"He seems like a cool dude," Mega said when I walked in.

"Yeah, he really is," I said with a bright smile.

"You seem happy. How are things with that shim?"

"Long story short, I ain't fucking with her no more." "Enough said. Well Jasmine is upstairs in her room," he said, before walking away. Walking up the stairs, I walked into Jasmine's room and as soon as she spotted me, she came running into my arms.

"Hey ma!"

"Hey baby girl!"

"I thought I wasn't gonna see you again," she said sadly.

"I know baby and I'm sorry, I was just handling some things."

"Yeah, Daddy told me, but I'm glad you're here now," she said, hugging me again. As we sat and caught up, she told me about school. At that moment, I couldn't think of any place I would rather be, other than with her. I was upset that it had taken me so long to get back to my baby, but I was glad that I did. I knew in my heart that I would never leave her again. After spending a few hours with my baby girl, it was time for her to get ready for bed, so I called Tyler to come get me. Sitting down in the living room, while Jasmine was in the shower, I was minding my business, scrolling through my newsfeed on Facebook, when Kaliah sat down next to me.

"Hey Ashley," she said, sounding fake as hell.

"What's up?" I asked, looking up from my phone. "Jason told me how good you've been, you know with Jasmine and everything."

Ok?"

"Well I just wanted to be sure that you weren't thinking about trying to take her back," she had the nerve to say.

"Where is this coming from, did Mega send you to ask me this?"

"No, I just know how some women can be."

"Well, I don't think that this is a conversation I need to be having with you. If Mega has any concerns or worries, he can come talk to me!" I snapped.

"Well I am his soon to be wife. I wasn't trying to be disrespectful, it's just we love Jasmine so much and would hate to see her go," she said.

"You wanna throw around the wife card, but you've only been in Jasmine's life for a fucking minute. So understand me when I say, there's nothing you can say to me pertaining to my child. There is only one chick that can pull that off and it's Cherish. I'mma need you to find ya place and stay in it," I snapped.

"What's going on?" Mega asked, walking into the living room.

"You better get your soon to be wife. And for future references, if you have any question for me, I would appreciate if you ask me yourself!" I snapped.

"What are you talking about?"

"She gon come down here talking bout am I gonna try and take Jasmine. Mega, you know how much I love my daughter. I know what I did before by bringing the cops here, but I would never snatch her from somewhere that she's obviously happy at."

"I didn't say you were gonna take her, the thought never crossed my mind. I mean of course when you get on your feet we'll have to work out some visitation, but we'll get there when we get there," he said.

"I don't know what she's so angry for, I just asked her a simple question," Kaliah said.

"But it wasn't your place to ask it!" I said. Before anyone could respond, the doorbell rang and I knew it was Tyler, so I grabbed my purse and walked out. I guess Mega was just as heated as I was because as soon as I walked out the door, he came out right after me.

"I don't know what's going on with Kaliah's ass, but it ain't her place to discuss anything with you," he said.

"I know now that you had nothing to do with it, so don't worry about it."

"Aight, but let me get out of here before I hurt her ass," he said, walking away.

Chapter Sixteen (Cherish)

I had so much fun here in the Bahamas, but I was so excited to be leaving. I was here for six days and I missed my babies so bad. I just want to kiss their chubby cheeks and have Jasmine talk me to death. I didn't realize how much the little things meant until I didn't have them. I closed my suitcase and wheeled it out to the living room. Me and Peter had really gotten to know each other on this trip. There were a few things that I didn't like about him, but for the most part, he was a complete sweetheart. When Peter was packed and ready, we headed to the lobby to meet up with everybody else. We had an hour before our flight left, so I hoped that nobody was late because the way I was missing my babies, they would fuck around and get left. When we got to the lobby, everyone was already waiting.

"Oh my God, we gotta come back here!" Camille said loudly.

"Why does she always have to be so loud?" Pete whispered.

"I'm loud too," I said. I was really starting to feel some type of way. I didn't like the way he talked about my friends. "I know, but we can work on that babe," he had the nerve to say.

"I love how I am, and any man I end up with will love how I am too," I said smartly.

"Oh come on babe, I know you're not mad," he said nonchalantly.

"You've been talking about my friends the whole trip Peter, but the weird part is, my friends act just like me."

"I just think there's a certain way that a woman should behave in public. I mean seriously, the way they were arguing in the limo, who does that type of stuff in front of company?" he laughed.

"That's the thing, we aren't company, we're family, there's a big difference," I said, shaking my head and walking away from him.

"What's wrong?" Camille asked me.

"I just don't think me and Peter will work," I said sadly.

"Why not?"

"We're too different. I mean I like him, but I don't want to have to change who I am just to accommodate him." "I feel you boo," she said, hugging me. When the van came, we all hopped in and headed to the airport. I could feel Peter staring at me, but I just ignored him. He kept sending me text messages apologizing, but I just ignored them. When we got to the airport, we quickly boarded the flight. I was happy that I didn't have to sit next to Peter's ass. To be honest, I wasn't even mad at him, I was hurt. I felt like if he could make fun of my friends, my family, the people that I love, then what would he say about me when I wasn't there.

After an almost four-hour long flight, I was ready to go home, see my babies and take my ass to sleep. When we got off the flight, everyone headed to their cars, and it was then that I remembered that I rode with Peter. Grabbing my bag, he placed it in the trunk of his car. Getting into the car, I put my seat all the way back and closed my eyes.

"Cherish, can we talk?" he asked.

"About what?"

"I understand you're upset with me, but I really don't know what I did."

"Seriously Peter?" I asked.

"Just talk to me."

"From the moment you met my friends, you turned your nose up at them. If it wasn't the weed, then it was the drinking. If not that then the partying or how loud they are." "How can you be mad at me because your friends are embarrassing?"

"They aren't embarrassing, you are!"

"You gotta be kidding me!"

"They were nothing but nice to you. Even though your ass was boring and kept a fucking mad face whenever you were around them, they still hung with you on the strength of me. But naw not you, ya ass couldn't do that!" I snapped.

"Calm down Cherish, you are being loud and irrational right now."

"Don't tell me to calm down, stop trying to change me. If I wanna curse, I'mma fucking curse!"

"Alright you can curse, I guess," he said, pissing me off even more. Instead of continuing to argue with him, I closed my eyes and faced the window. When we got to my house, I wasted no time jumping out the car and walking up to my door.

"I'mma call you, ok?"

"Listen Peter, I like you, but I don't think we should be anything more than friends. They are more than my friends, they are my family, and if you can't accept them then you can't accept me," I said before walking into the house and closing the door. As soon as I got in the house, I took a shower and then called Mega to bring me my babies. As I sat on my couch, waiting for them to come, I got the phone call I'd been waiting for since going to the Bahamas.

"Hello?" I answered.

"Hey Cherish, this is Marcus Green. I was hoping you'd answer."

"Is everything ok?"

"Yes ma'am, everything is done and I think it's to your liking."

"Oh my God, I'm so happy!" I screamed.

"So when can you come check it out?" he asked.

"I can meet you there tomorrow morning."

"That's perfect, does ten work for you?"

"It sure does."

"Alright, see you then boss lady," he said, before hanging up. I knew when I told them I wanted it done, but I didn't think they would be able to do everything I wanted in such little time. I could hear my door unlock, and I knew it was the nanny, Evelyn.

"Oh my gosh, you're back!" she said, walking in with a ton of groceries.

"Yeah, I'm so happy to be home, but we had a great time," I said, grabbing some bags out of her hands. After we put all the bags into the kitchen, she gave me a big hug. I really missed her because she's become like family since I hired her.

"Well you go get some rest, while I put these groceries away."

"No, I can put them away, you go sit down. While I'm doing that, I'll tell you all about the trip," I said laughing. While

I put the groceries away, I told her about me and Peter breaking up, and she wasn't the least bit surprised.

"Honey, that man put the B in bougie," she said, causing me to laugh.

"I know, but I just couldn't accept the way he treated them, I was really hurt."

"I still think you and Jason are meant for each other," she said seriously.

"He's engaged, haven't you heard?"

"Well I for one don't think he's happy. The other day, we took the kids to the park and I knew that girl wanted to go with us, but instead, he strapped the kids in and left her just standing at the door," she said laughing.

"You ain't right," I said, shaking my head. We talked for a little longer before the doorbell rang and I jumped up to go greet my babies. Opening the door, I grabbed one of the car seats from Mega and gave my baby girl all the kisses, then I grabbed Jr. and kissed him all over his chubby face.

"Well what about me?" Jasmine pouted.

"Oh how could I forget about my big baby girl," I said, grabbing her and placing kisses all over her face.

"I missed you so much ma," she said happily.

"I missed you too."

"Did you miss me enough to take me with you next time?"

"Well I wanna get married there, it was so beautiful. So yeah, I'll take you next time."

"You getting married?" Mega asked.

"I mean eventually, I ain't gonna stay single forever," I said laughing.

"I guess, but real talk, I'm glad you had fun Lil Mama," he said, causing me to blush. Since breaking up, it was rare that he called me little mama anymore, so when he did, I couldn't help but feel those same butterflies I felt when we first met.

"I got some good news!" I said happily.

"What's up?" he asked.

"Well I didn't want to tell too many people, but I've been making plans to open up an outreach program. I bought the property a few months ago and the contractors just finished renovating it. Now all I have to do is get the furniture and it's done," I said proudly.

"Oh Cherish, I'm so proud of you baby!" Evelyn said, hugging me. She was one of the people who knew of my plans.

"Why didn't you tell me about this?" he asked.

"I don't know, I mean we don't really talk often, outside of talking about the kids," I said honestly.

"Ummmm, I'mma put the kids to bed, come on Jasmine," Evelyn said before walking out of the room.

"I could have helped you," he said, sounding left out.

"Mega, you are about to be married. I can't keep depending on you to do everything, not anymore."

"Married or not, I got ya back no matter what, and you know that."

"I know, but I wanted to do this on my own. I like this whole independent single thing," I said laughing.

"Yeah, I see. What about you and white chocolate?" he said laughing.

"Hahaha, real funny nigga. But we're just friends, like I told you before," I said, not wanting to give him too much information about what happened.

"Yeah aight, but let me get out of here," he said, before heading to the door. Walking behind him so I could lock it, he turned around abruptly and I bumped into him. For some reason when our bodies touched, I got nervous as hell. He was so close I could feel his breath on my forehead.

"I like this whole independence vibe you got going, it looks good on you," he said sexily before walking out. Closing and locking the door, I leaned on the door when he left, so I could catch my breath. I wasn't sure if he was trying to turn me on or if it just came naturally for him, but he had a bitch dripping. I had to tell myself over and over that he was engaged to be married, and that was one line I would never cross.

Chapter Seventeen (Mega)

After dropping the kids off, I headed home. It had been days since Kaliah stepped to Ashley and aside from sleeping there, I had been out all day every day, trying to avoid her ass. Me and the kids would either go to Mama Betty's house, and I made sure I called before going, or I would just take them to the park and other places to tire them out. When I did come home at night, she would attempt to talk to me, but I wasn't tryna hear shit she had to say. She was completely out of pocket and that shit was unacceptable. Pulling up to my house, I was finally tired of being upset with her, so when I walked in, I planned to just tell her how I felt and she could take that shit how she wanted. When I walked into the house, Kaliah was sitting on the couch crying, which surprised me because she rarely cried.

"Why you sitting in the dark crying?" I asked.

"You've been treating me like shit for days, I said sorry."

"What were you thinking asking her some shit like that!" I snapped.

"I don't know, I just know how happy Jasmine makes you."

"Listen, I love you, but when it comes to my kids and their mothers, I need you to stay out of it."

"But I will be their stepmother."

"That doesn't give you permission to ask questions pertaining to our children. Anything I feel I want to ask, I can ask myself," I said, shaking my head.

"I just want to be involved Jason," she said.

"You are involved, but there needs to be boundaries."

"I understand, please tell me you forgive me."

"I forgave you as soon as I saw you in here crying, Kaliah. I don't want to see you cry, but I need you to respect me and the mother of my children," I said sternly, before picking her up and carrying her upstairs to the bedroom. Laying her down, she grabbed my neck and kissed me hungrily. I watched as she closed her eyes and let a soft moan leave her lips. Breaking the kiss, I grabbed her left breast and licked her nipple lightly. Reaching her hand down my back, she grabbed my shirt and pulled it off. Getting up, I quickly took off my sneaker and pants, before climbing back on top of her and putting her nipple back into my mouth. Placing my fingers on top of her opening, I rubbed her clit until she begged me to fuck her. Sliding two fingers inside of her, I fingered her until she let out a scream and creamed all over my hand.

"Please fuck me!" she begged.

"You want me to fuck you?" I asked, while sucking her nipple.

"Sssssssss, yes please!" she screamed. Flipping her over, I rammed my dick into her center roughly. Grabbing her hair, I fed her all of my dick, while she screamed out in pain and pleasure. I could feel her trying to get away from me, so I gripped her hips tightly and pulled her back.

"Where you going, I thought you wanted this dick."

"Slow down baby," she said.

"Naw, you wanted me to fuck you, right?" I asked, while still banging her back out.

"I'm bout to cum!" she screamed. After a few more pumps, I felt her pussy clamp my dick, before she exploded all over me. As I continued to fuck her, she came a few more times before I felt my nut building up. When I reached my peak, I pulled my dick out of her and nutted on her ass.

"Why you always got to do that?" she asked with an attitude. Ignoring her, I got up to get her a warm rag. When I came back, she was still tooted up, waiting for me to clean her off. Taking the rag, I gently wiped her off, before climbing back into the bed. I could tell she still had an attitude because I didn't nut in her.

"So you just gonna ignore me?" she asked.

"Don't fuck up a good night Kaliah, I'm tired," I said, before turning over. I actually wanted to go a few more rounds, until she gave me attitude, now I was turned off and ready for bed. Ever since I proposed to her, for some reason she seemed pressed to have a child. Don't get me wrong I love kids and I wouldn't mind giving her a child, but not right now. That shit was out of the question, I still had toddlers in diapers.

"I don't wanna argue with you so I'mma just leave it alone," she said. The next morning, I woke up to a text message from Camille, asking me if I could call her.

"What's up Cam?"

"Hey, my bad for calling you so early."

"You good, everything ok?"

"Yeah, do you think we can meet up?"

"When, right now?" I asked.

"Yeah, if you can," she said, not sounding like herself. After hanging up with her, I hopped in the shower, got dressed and headed over to her house. When I pulled up, the kids were outside playing and she was sitting on the step. "So what's up?" I asked.

"Well, I need advice from a man," she said.

"Aight," I said, hoping she didn't ask me no bullshit.

"I'm pregnant," she blurted out.

"Ok, congratulations?" I asked, confused.

"I don't know."

"This is Mark's baby, right?" I asked.

"Oh you tried it nigga, yeah this his baby!" she snapped.

"Ok, so what's the problem?"

"I found out before the trip to the Bahamas, but I don't think he wants any more kids."

"Yeah he does, he talks about it all the time," I said.

"Alright damn, I don't want any more kids right now."

"Wow, I don't know what to say."

"How do you think he would feel if I told him?" she asked.

"I think he would be pissed. I mean you're not thinking about aborting it, are you?"

"Of course not. I mean I love children, but he doesn't really help me. I have to do everything myself when it comes to them, I just want some help."

"So tell him that. I think if he knew how you felt, he would make some changes."

"I don't know. I just don't want him to think that I don't want the baby, when the truth is I just don't wanna do it all by myself."

"I understand. How about you talk to him and if he doesn't understand what you're tryna say, then I'll holla at him."

"Thank you!" she said.

"You straight, but now I need a favor from you."

"Oh lawd," she said, sounding stressed already.

"I just want you to hang with Kaliah, even if it's once. I mean she's feeling real left out of the crew."

"Nigga that's cuz she ain't in this crew!" "I just need that one favor."

"Man, I would have to talk to Cherish, and even then, you know I don't do fake."

"I know, but do something that doesn't involve much talking, like go shopping or something."

"Aight Mega, damn!" she said, before calling the kids in and slamming the door in my face. When I was almost home, Camille called me and let me know that Cherish said it was cool and that I could tell Kaliah for her. When I got home, I rushed inside to find Kaliah in the living room, doing yoga. I swear this girl was the healthiest person I knew.

"Hey babe!" she said happily.

"What you doing tomorrow?" I asked.

"Nothing, I'm off," she said.

"Aight, well Camille wanted you to go shopping with her tomorrow."

"Seriously, I didn't think she liked me!" she said excited.

"I told you they didn't have a problem with you."

"Ok well tell her I would love to go," she said smiling.

Chapter Eighteen (Cherish)

Pulling up to my building, I was nervous and excited as I walked in with Marcus. I had seen a lot of their work on Facebook, so I knew it would be beautiful, I just hoped they understood what I wanted.

"Hey Marcus," I said, shaking his hand.

"How are you Cherish?"

"I'm great, excited," I said with a smile.

"Well I won't keep you in suspense any longer," he said, before unlocking and opening the door. When I walked in, I was in complete shock, it was beautiful. Empty of course, but beautiful. Everything was perfect. As I walked through the building, I couldn't find anything that I didn't love about what they had been able to do in such a short period of time. After seeing the entire building, I handed him the check and gave him a hug. I couldn't thank him enough for the work he did. A lot of times when you're a woman coming to a man for work, they try and give you some bullshit job, but he did what I wanted. After he was gone, I pulled out my phone to call Camille, but before I could dial her number, she was calling me.

"Guess what!" I said when I answered.

"What?"

"The building is complete, so I need you to furnish it!" I said excitedly. I always told her that she should do interior design because of all the compliments she got on her house.

"Oh my God, congrats!"

"My bad, I forgot that you called me first, so what's up?"

"Girl Mega's ass asked me if I could hang out with Kaliah," she said, surprising me.

"Why would he ask you of all people to do that?"

"He kinda gave me advice on this situation, so I owed him a favor."

"Oh well if you asking me how I feel about you hanging with her, then the answer is I could give zero fucks, as long as when I call you answer," I said laughing.

"You already know, but let me call you back so I can give this nigga the ok," she said before hanging up. I honestly didn't feel upset that she was gonna chill with her because I knew how Camille was. She couldn't stand a shiesty bitch and that's exactly what Kaliah was. After looking at my soon to be outreach program/group home. Now that I was one step closer to making my dream a reality, I headed to see Mark and Kasan. They told me that they would love to invest in my program a few months ago, I just hoped they still felt the same way. I mean I planned on getting grants for the program, but that could take months, so I would use whatever they gave me to hold me over until the government grants kicked in. Yeah, I had my own money, but that's what the government is for, so why not milk them for all I can, especially since it was for a good cause. Pulling up to Mark's club, I parked and then called Shana.

"Hey boo, I need a favor," I said when she answered.

"Damn, can I get a hi or something before you start begging," she said laughing.

"My bad, hey boo. Now I need a favor."

"What's up?"

"You think you can print me out some colorful fliers to promote the outreach program?"

"Of course I can. Are you still calling it Camden's Safe Haven?" she said. I couldn't believe that she remembered. Hell, even I forgot that I had come up with that name last year while we were having some girl time.

"Yeah, I will text you when I get a number for it. I'm supposed to call Comcast tomorrow."

"Alright, just let me know and congrats boo."

"Thank you," I said, hanging up. When I got off the phone with her, I hopped out the car and walked straight into the club. Everyone knew who I was because of Mega, so I usually had no problems.

"Damn, who you?" some ugly ass nigga with funky breath asked all in my face.

"Not interested!" I said, walking past him. When I got upstairs, Mark and Kasan were laughing hard as hell.

"Why you play that man out like that?" Kasan asked.

"Please, he played my nose out, talking to me with his breath smelling like ass crack crunch. Ugh, niggas need to do better," I said, sitting down.

"You so damn mean these days," Mark said.

"I get it from y'all wives."

"Probably. Shit, Camille been mean as hell lately, with her pregnant ass," Mark said laughing.

"Wait, pregnant?" I asked, confused.

"I assumed you knew. Shit, she thinks she's keeping that shit from me, like I don't clock her periods."

"You clock her periods?" I asked.

"All niggas do," he shrugged.

"I wonder why she didn't tell me?" I asked out loud to myself.

"I'm wondering the same thing, but if she don't tell me soon, I'mma beat her ass," he said before getting up and handing me two checks for fifty thousand.

"Wow, I didn't expect you guys to give me this much."

"We all for giving back to the community. Too many of these young kids are dying cuz they ain't got nowhere to turn but to the streets," Kasan said.

"I really appreciate this," I said, hugging them both. Instead of leaving when I got the check, I ended up staying longer than I'd planned. Right when I was about to say goodbye, in walked Mega's ugly fine ass with his thot ass fiancé.

"Oh shit, am I interrupting something?" he asked.

"Nope, I was just leaving," I said, before grabbing my purse and standing.

"Aight Cherish, hit us up if you need anything else."

"I really appreciate it."

"Damn, what they help you with, maybe I can help too."

"They gave me a donation for the outreach program," I said nonchalantly.

"What the fuck Cherish, damn. I said I would help you if you needed it."

"Yes Cherish, whatever you need, we don't mind helping you," Kaliah said.

"I don't need anything from Y'ALL," I said, all while staring at Jason with hurt eyes. When did they become an us and a we? Last I checked they weren't married yet.

"Hello Cherish," Kaliah said brightly. I don't know what's wrong with this girl, but it had to be something if she was speaking to me as if we were besties. Since I've been trying to become a better me, I waved at her and kept it pushing. Fast walking to the car, I couldn't get there fast enough. Everything in my body wanted to be petty, but I refused to let her get to me. Pulling off, I headed to Camille's house. As soon as I got there, I wasted no time parking and knocking on the door.

"Damn girl, banging on my door like you the police!" she snapped.

"Bitch, you pregnant!"

"What the fuck, Mega! Damn that nigga can't hold water."

"Mega? You told that nigga, but didn't tell me!"

"Come inside and stop making a scene drama queen," she said, causing me to laugh. I quickly stopped when I remembered that I was supposed to be mad at her.

"So does Shante know?"

"Nobody knows except Mega, I just needed advice."

"From Mega?" I said, confused.

"Look, I've just been feeling real confused about this pregnancy. I don't wanna bring another child into this world, just to have to do shit alone again."

"What you mean alone, Mark is there."

"Girl, he always on the run. I had dreams too and just when I start looking into the whole interior designer thing, I find out I'm pregnant again, which pushes me back another few years," she said teary-eyed.

"Awwwww boo, regardless of whether he helps you or not, single working women make it work every day, so I know you can. Shit, get a nanny," I said honestly.

"I was thinking about it, but I don't know. Mark is big on not having people in the house and me taking care of our kids like a mom should."

"No, the parents are supposed to handle shit together. If he isn't helping you bare the weight of something you guys mutually created, then he needs to shut the hell up and let you get some help in here."

"You're right, I'mma just tell him I'm pregnant tonight."

"Girl, he's the one that told me you were pregnant," I said laughing.

"He what!"

"Talking bout he tracks ya period, and if you didn't tell him soon, he was gonna beat ya ass."

"What the fuck, I swore he didn't know. That nigga gonna kick my ass," she said laughing.

"How far are you?"

"I'm almost four months," she said, shaking my head.

"You ain't even showing."

"Girl, you a lie!" she said, standing up. She lifted up her shirt and sure enough, there sat her round bulging belly.

"Oh wow, you big as hell," I said laughing.

"Fuck you!"

"I love you too."

"Anyways, I ordered some furniture for the outreach program based off the colors you have. I know you wanted couches, bunk beds and the stuff for the offices," she said.

"Thank you so much boo!" I said, hugging her. I really appreciate everything that everyone was doing to help me.

"No problem, you know I got ya back."

"I know, but I'm bout to head home," I said, before getting up to leave.

Chapter Nineteen (Mega)

I was happy as shit to be getting some time away from Kaliah. Don't get me wrong I love spending time with her, but lately she's been doing too much. I understand she wants to be involved. I also understand that she doesn't have any children on her own, and she wants some, but damn, she hitting a nigga hard with all this shit at once. I know that she feels left out, which is why I asked Cam to chill with her. I didn't think she would actually agree, but I'm glad she did because I was willing to do anything to get this chick off my back. As I sat playing *Call of Duty* on my Ps4, my phone started ringing. I started not to answer that shit, but when I saw it was Camille, I said fuck it.

"Yo!"

"Hey Mega, I was just calling you to let you know to get dressed. I'm bringing Mark and all the girls are bringing their men."

"I thought y'all were having a girls' day," I said, mad as hell. I was gonna order some pizza, play some games, shit I didn't get to do around Kaliah's ass.

"I want to tell Mark about the pregnancy. I think I would feel better if all of our friends were there." "So you inviting Cherish?" I asked.

"I did invite her, but she already knows about the pregnancy. Plus, she's busy planning the grand opening of her center, so I don't think she'll make it."

"Oh, she's having a party and ain't send a nigga no invite."

"She hasn't sent out the invites yet."

"Oh aight, and I'mma need for you and ya girls to be cordial tonight."

"I'm always cordial," she said, sounding offended.

"Yeah aight, come on," I said.

"Aight aight, damn, we'll be nice," she said with an attitude, before hanging up in my ear. Walking upstairs, I went to tell Kaliah about the change of plans.

"I'm so excited about tonight!" she said excitedly.

"Yeah about that, Camille changed it and we're all meeting for dinner."

"Oh, that's even better. So we're gonna double date basically," she said with a smile.

"Something like that," I said laughing. I could never understand why she was so pressed to be around people that didn't fuck with her like that. After we were both dressed, we headed out to the Cheesecake Factory to meet up with the rest of the group. Pulling up to the restaurant, I waited as Kaliah checked her make-up like four times.

"You ready?" I asked, getting impatient.

"Yeah, I guess I'm just nervous."

"It's just dinner Kaliah, nothing serious," I said. When we walked into the restaurant, everyone was already there, including Cherish. I didn't want her to feel some type of way, so I tried to act like I wasn't surprised to see her there. Walking around the table, I gave daps to the niggas and hugs to the ladies.

"You're late," Camille said.

"My bad," I said laughing.

"It's all good. Cherish ordered for you, but we didn't know what Kaliah liked," Camille said with a smirk.

"What you order me?"

"Ummmmm the firecracker salmon for ya app, and the hibachi steak with mashed potatoes and asparagus," Cherish said.

"Thanks," I said. I could feel Kaliah staring at me, so I grabbed her hand to reassure her that I was there with her and no one else. As we waited for the waitress to come back around and take Kaliah's order, the tension was thick and everyone was quiet. By the time the waitress came back, she was bringing out the appetizers.

"I didn't order," Kaliah said.

"What would you like?" the waitress asked.

"I'll have the loaded baked potato tots," she said with a smile.

"And for your main course?"

"No, that's all I want," she said.

"Ok I'll put that right in."

"Is that all you're gonna eat?" Shante asked her.

"Yeah, I have to maintain my figure for the wedding," Kaliah said with a smile.

"Hmmmp," Shante said.

"Well, I have an announcement to make," Camille said with a smile.

"Well spit it out girl!" Shana said laughing.

"Damn, chill out… I'm pregnant," she announced."Wait what, how far along? When? What?" Shante said.

"I'm sixteen weeks," she said, while staring at Mark.

"Congrats bro!" I said happily.

"Yeah, thanks," Mark replied with an attitude.

"Well congratulations, Camille. I'm so happy that you trusted me enough to be a part of your announcement."

"Ummmmmm, you're welcome."

"I'm not trying to steal your shine, but since I have you ladies here, I had a question," she said. I had no fucking clue what she was about to ask them.

"What's up?" Queesha asked.

"I wanted to know if you, Camille, would be my maid of honor and the rest of you could be bridesmaids?"

"Are you fucking serious!" Shante snapped.

"Well I don't have any sisters or family members, so I thought it would be cool. I mean we are getting to know each other."

"So you want me to be in your wedding?" Cherish asked.

"I would love it if you came, but I was referring to the other women, as far as being in it. I know it would be weird if you were in it," she said laughing.

"I'mma take my food to go, but whatever they agree to is ok with me," Cherish said, getting up and walking away.

"So what do you girls say?"

"I'mma act like you didn't just say that crazy fairytale shit!" Camille said.

"Why would any of us what to be involved in your side chick wedding!" Shante snapped.

"Shante, cut it out!" Kasan snapped.

"What, I'm just telling her the truth," Shante shrugged.

"I'm not a side chick. When I got with Mega, him and Cherish weren't together."

"She isn't my side chick, y'all need to cut that shit out. She wants y'all to be a part of the wedding. She's been nothing but cool to y'all messy asses!" I snapped.

"Can we just go?" Kaliah asked.

"Just give me a minute," I said, before getting up to catch up with Cherish.

"Yo, you need to talk to ya fucking friends!"

"Excuse me?" she asked with an attitude.

"I'm serious Cherish. That girl ain't been nothing but nice to them."

"Have I not been cordial with her?"

"You have, but I'm talking about the rest of them."

"Well you need to talk to them, not me!"

"They're doing this shit because of you."

"What the fuck, they are grown women Mega. I can't control their behavior and even if I could, you got some fucking nerve asking me to!"

"So what am I supposed to do?" I asked, feeling fucking defeated.

"I don't know, but the first thing you need to do is stop tryna force that girl on MY FRIENDS, MY CREW, MY SISTERS, it ain't never gonna happen. I get you replacing me as ya girl, but you can't replace me as their friend and try to move that bitch in. I guess they got more loyalty than ya ass!" she snapped, before walking out of the restaurant. Walking back to the table, I watched and listened as Camille and Kaliah had a heated conversation.

"I don't understand why y'all are attacking me right now. He's about to be my husband, which means I will be in this group, whether y'all like it or not."

"No, you will be his wife, but you will never be our friend because that job already belongs to Cherish."

"Come on now Camille, you totally outta pocket!" I snapped.

"What you want me to do, keep lying to the girl? My loyalty lies with Cherish. Shit, all of our loyalty lies with her, you lucky if I even show up!" she said before walking away.

"I'll talk to her. She'll be at the wedding, but she ain't gonna be no bridesmaid nigga, that's asking a bit much from my wife," Mark said.

"Man, I ain't know shit about this whole bridesmaid shit," I said, shaking my head. After Mark and Camille left, so did everyone else. During the car ride home, no words were spoken.

Chapter Twenty (Ashley)

It's been a couple of weeks since I'd been staying with Tyler and I could honestly say I was falling in love with him. Why haven't had sex yet and it was starting to piss me off and make me feel self-conscious. I wasn't sure why he hadn't made a pass at me, I tried everything. I walk around the house in skimpy clothes, I'm doing things that I know would turn the normal nigga on but for some reason, it ain't working with him. Maybe I'm losing it. Walking into the living room wearing one of his t-shirts, like usual, he barely paid me any mind. Walking into the kitchen, I grabbed a soda and took the walk of shame back to the bedroom. When I walked back past him, he grabbed my arm and pulled me on to his lap.

"What you doing?" I asked with a smile.

"I should be asking you the same shit," he said, while rubbing my thighs.

"What you talkin bout?" I asked, trying to play stupid.

"Stop playing with me ma. You walking round here fucking naked, bendin that fat ass over in front of me." "You don't want it, so why does it matter?" I said, pouting.

"Who told you I didn't want it? Just because I got control over my dick, don't mean I don't see what you doing, and it don't mean that I don't want ya sexy ass."

"So what's the problem?" I asked.

"I like you, I'm falling for you hard, but I know what you're used to and I want something different with you."

"What do you want from me?"

"I want you to be my wife," he said seriously.

"Do you really wanna marry me?"

"Hell yeah. I got mad love for you and your daughter," he said. Last weekend, I let him meet Jasmine for the first time. It wasn't nothing serious, but I introduced them and let him go with us to the park, just to show Mega and her that I planned to have him around. It was crazy because Mega accepted him and I thought for sure that he would be a problem, but he seemed to like Tyler and so did Jasmine. Ever since the park, we had been hanging out every weekend with Tyler, supervised by Mega of course, but he didn't hover over us. He always made sure to give me and Jasmine privacy, even if we were in his house or in a public place.

"You don't even know me well enough."

"Who are you to tell me how well I know you? Fuck knowing your past, I know your heart and I love it," he said with so much passion. Straddling his lap, he kissed me for the first time. With one hand gripping my ass and the other hand holding the back of my head, he kissed me with so much love and lust that he caused my whole body to shake.

"I want you," I said hungrily.

"Naw, this ain't about sex," he said.

"Ya mouth talking that shit, but ya dick begging to be inside me," I whispered into his ear. I wasn't trying to hear shit he was talking. Lifting slightly off him, I pulled his dick out of his basketball shorts and pulled my panties to the side. I already knew he was packing because as bad as I was feening for him, I knew everything about his dick, without him even showing me. Sitting on his dick slowly, I laid my head on his chest and just sat there for a minute, savoring how good he felt inside of me.

"You ok?" he asked, kissing my cheek.

"I'm ok, you just feel so good to me," I said with a light smile. Lifting up, I slowly gyrated on his dick as my juices instantly began to flow. He grabbed my waist and slowly lifted me up, making me bounce on his dick.

"You know I love you, right Ash?" he moaned. Niggas always loved me when they were inside me, so instead of getting excited about him professing his love for me, I just closed my eyes, bit my bottom lip and took that dick like only I could. As I felt his dick get even harder and his body stiffen, I tightened my muscles and came hard on his dick shortly after he came long and hard inside of me. As I laid on his chest with his dick still inside of me, he kissed me all over my face, while rubbing my back. I'd never been shown so much love and care after sex and I was loving it. As he played in my hair, I dozed off with a smile on my face.

"Ash!" I heard Tyler yell. Jumping up out of my sleep I realized that he must have carried me into the bedroom.

"Yeah!" I screamed, while rubbing my eyes.

"Your phone been ringing off the hook!" he said. Getting out of bed, I walked into the living room to grab my phone. As soon as I saw Tyler, I couldn't help the smile that came on my face. As we stared into each other's eyes like love sick puppies, my phone began to ring again. As I reached my hand out to grab my phone, he pulled it back and held it over his head.

"Gimmie my phone, Ty!"

"Gimmie a kiss and I'll think about it," he said with a smile. Leaning over, I gave him a quick peck on the lips and tried to grab my phone.

"I gave you a kiss," I laughed.

"Uh huh, kiss me like you love me," he said. Reaching over, I kissed him with everything I had inside of me. After almost an hour, he had finally given me my phone back, because that kiss led to us fucking again.

"You play too much!" I said, out of breath from the work out he'd just given me.

"You love it!" he said, handing me my phone. As I looked through my phone, I had a bunch of missed calls from Jayda and a couple from Jasmine. Ignoring Jayda's calls, I called Jasmine back.

"Hey baby!" I said when she answered.

"Hey, Mama Ashley. You wanna come have dinner with us?" she asked.

"Who's us?" I asked. I was praying that she didn't say Kaliah because ever since our last conversation, I couldn't stand her ass.

"Me and mommy," she said, referring to Cherish. Yeah she called her mom and for a minute, I was angry and hurt, but I decided that instead of being upset, I would focus all my energy on making her love me again. I had to gain her trust back and show her that I was here to stay. "What did Cherish say?"

"She said you could come. We're having a girls' night out," she said happily.

"Let me speak to her Jasmine."

"Hello?" I heard Cherish say.

"Hey ummmm, Jasmine said you were cool with me coming?"

"Oh yeah, she wants to see you, so I told her to invite you," she said, surprising me.

"Are you sure?" I asked.

"Yeah, like I said, Jasmine wants you here and I'm fine with that."

"Wow, thank you so much. When should I come?"

"You can meet us at the nail salon on Federal St. in an hour."

"Ok, I'll be there. Thank you again, Cherish."

"No problem," she said, before hanging up.

"Can you drop me off?"

"Naw," he said, surprising me.

"Oh, you have something to do?"

"No," he said, before getting up and walking towards the garage door. Following behind him, I was curious as hell. When I walked into the garage, right beside his 2015 Dodge Charger was an all-white Audi. When I looked at him for confirmation that this was mine, he simply tossed me the keys. I wasn't sure how he could afford this car on a cop's salary, but in that moment, that was the last thing on my mind.

"You didn't have to do this, but thank you so much babe!" I screamed, jumping into his arms.

"Man, I was tired of being ya chauffeur," he said laughing.

"Whatever!" I said, still hugging him. After checking out my car, I went to take a shower and get dressed. When I was done, I kissed my man and headed out to meet my baby. With my music blasting, I drove to the nail salon. When I pulled up, I watched as Jasmine and Cherish hopped out of her all black Lexus GX truck. She was definitely a bad bitch and I could most definitely see what Mega saw in her. She looked confident, she was beautiful and she had a nice little petite body.

"Hey Mama Ashley," Jasmine said, hugging me."Hey baby, and hey Cherish."

"What's up, I see you pushing that Audi girl, that thing hot," Cherish said sincerely. Me and Cherish had an understanding, which allowed us to be cool. We weren't friends, but we respected each other and no longer had any bad blood, our main objective was Jasmine. I had been by her house to play with Jasmine a few times when she was with her and not Mega, and she always treated me nicely.

"Thank you," I said, blushing. It had been so long since a female actually gave me a genuine compliment about anything. It was hard for me to even accept it because I was so used to bitches hating me, but with Cherish, she was a bad bitch herself, so she had no reason to hate. Walking into the salon, we waited until it was our turn and when it was, we sat in the pedi chair and let the massager relax us. They even had a little cute Hello Kitty chair for Jasmine to sit in, and she really felt like she was a big kid because of it.

"I think it's time for acrylic," she said seriously.

"Pshhh, little girl you thought wrong," Cherish said, serious as a heart attack.

"Yeah, leave the thinking to us adults," I said laughing.

"Well it was worth a try," Jasmine said with a shrug.

"Yeah, you tried it alright," Cherish said, laughing hard. As the three of us got our toes done, we talked with Jasmine about school, a boy she liked, and how her grades needed to be her main focus.

"Daddy says I don't need a boyfriend because I got him, but that's nasty, I heard he can go to jail for that."

"For what?" I asked, nervous as hell.

"You know."

"Hell naw we don't know."

"If you marry your daughter or son you can go to jail," she said, causing me and Cherish to let out a sigh of relief.

"Yeah, you can't do that," I said, shaking my head. I was so happy with how things were going. Yeah, I got to see her every weekend, but she still wasn't comfortable with me. We talked, but not about the good mommy daughter stuff like boys and mean girls. It seems like with Cherish here, she was coming out of her shell.

"So this what the fuck you been up to?" I heard someone say from behind me. When I turned around, sure enough it was Jayda's ass.

"Jayda, I know you see me with my daughter, please go away."

"Man, fuck that. I've been calling you for weeks, so you can imagine how surprised I was to get a phone call talking bout my Ashley is driving a brand new Audi and hanging in the nail place with my man's baby mama!"

"Lawd, you still fucking crazy and delusional, huh? Jasmine, baby, let's go," Cherish said, getting up from the drying machine and walking out with Jasmine.

"I can't believe you hanging with the fucking enemy!"

"She's your enemy, not mine. I don't have a problem with her. Shit, I feel bad for even playing a part in your crazy plans!" I snapped, before turning to leave.

"So you really ain't fucking with me no more?" she asked, actually sounding hurt. Instead of answering her, I continued to my car. When I got outside, Cherish had just finished putting Jasmine in the car.

"You good Ashley?" Cherish asked.

"I'm ok, just get Jasmine home, please. I don't want her seeing this crazy shit," I said.

"Alright, please call me when you get home," she said, before rolling her eyes at Jayda and pulling off.

"Look, I'm sorry for putting my hands on you." "Which time?"

"Every time. Seriously, I'm sorry," she said.

"I accept your apology, but I have to go," I said, before jumping in my car. As I started the ignition, Jayda walked away. I guess for once in her life, she finally got the hint and understood when she was no longer wanted. When I got home, I told Tyler about what went down. He was certain that it wasn't over and to be honest, I felt like he was right.

Chapter Twenty-One (Cherish)

As I walked through my outreach center, I couldn't help but fall in love with it. Everything was finished. It was furnished and I even had a few teenagers that were anticipating it opening. I had just hired my last residential supervisor, who was a nice middle aged lady with her masters in social work. All together I had hired sixteen employees, but most of them were volunteers, who jumped at the chance to work for me. I had been handing out fliers everywhere for over a month and in less than thirty minutes, my grand opening party will be starting. I had so many people from the city of Camden coming out to support me that I'd never even heard of until now.

"It's beautiful in here boo!" Camille said, hugging me.

"Yeah, it is. Thank you so much for all your help."

"No problem, so did you invite Mega?"

"Yeah, I sent him and his crazy fiancé an invite, but you know I ain't fucking with him like that."

"Damn, still?"

"Hell yeah, he pissed me off, stepping to me on some bullshit."

"Yeah, he was wrong for that shit. I mean it ain't ya fault we don't like the bitch and it ain't shit you or him can do about it."

"Exactly, but me sending them the invite was basically a peace offering, so he better show the fuck up."

"You know he wouldn't miss your big night."

"I guess."

"Anyways, we'll have drinks, finger food and music. It will start outside and when you cut the ribbon, everyone will come inside and the party will begin," she said excitedly.

"Alright and did everyone rsvp?"

"Just about everyone did, so it will be pretty packed."

"I'm nervous as hell."

"Don't be, this is a huge accomplishment, and the community is proud of you. Oh, plus you look too good to be nervous," she said, hugging me.

"Thank you, you look beautiful too."

"Alright, now that we got that out the way, you need to get out of here so I can finish. Go home and touch up your make-up," she said. When I got back home, the kids were already dressed and ready. They looked so adorable in their dresses and Jr. in his little suit. After touching up my make-up, I was ready to head back with the kids. As soon as I opened the door, I saw a beautiful black limo waiting for me. I couldn't believe that Camille would do this for me, but before I could get overly excited, the window rolled down and there sat Peter.

"What are you doing here?"

"I couldn't miss this," he said with a smile.

"Thank you, but…."

"No buts, please get in the limo," he begged.

"Yeah mommy, I wanna ride in the limo too."

"Uh huh girl, you come on in the car with me and the twins," the nanny said.

"But I wanted to go," Jasmine pouted. Walking away, she got into the car with the nanny.

"You heard what she said, so get in," Peter said laughing. Getting into the limo, I refused to be mad at Peter for his little pop up act. Tonight was my night. I wasn't gonna let anyone ruin it, so I sat back and enjoyed the ride. The closer we got to the center, the more nervous I became. However when we pulled up, I got the surprise of a lifetime. Outside, in front of the center, stood about two hundred people.

"Oh my God, is that NBC news!" I screamed. When the limo pulled up in front of the center, Peter got out and opened my door. Peter held my hand and helped me out. Taking a deep breath, I climbed out of the limo. As soon as I was out the limo, everyone began to clap and cheer. As I looked around at the people I loved most surrounding me, I couldn't help but smile.

"Ms. Daniels, what inspired you to open this outreach program?" a reporter asked.

"Not too long ago, I was a child in need of saving, but at the end of the day, I had no one to turn to. Your teachers say the they can help you, but the minute you let them know of anything happening, they call DYFS, and nine times out of ten, you end up worst off than you were originally. I was scared because I heard all the stories about foster care and foster homes. Well this place right here is for the girl being abused who doesn't want to go home, this place is for the boy who doesn't want to join a gang, or who doesn't want to go home to an abusive father."

"So did you go into foster care, because you turned out great?" the reporter said with a smile.

"Thank you, but no I didn't, I had someone that loved me enough to save me, and I will always be grateful to him," I said, while looking at Mega with a smile.

"Well, let's cut this ribbon, shall we?" the mayor said. Walking over to the entrance of my building, Camille handed me some massive sized scissors and after posing for a few pictures, I cut the ribbon. As soon as we were inside, the party started. The music was low and nice. All I had to do now was ditch Peter's ass, then everything would be perfect.

"Congratulations Lil Mama," I heard Mega say.

"Thank you," I said, turning around, facing him. It was like I was stuck; he was so damn fine in his little cardigan.

"Hmmmmmm," Peter said, clearing his throat.

"Jason, you remember Peter."

"Yeah, what's up, but I wanted to know if I could have this dance?"

"Yes, you can," I said with a smile, before walking away with him. As we began to slow dance, we continued to talk.

"You looked like you needed saving."

"Yeah, I did. I didn't even invite his ass."

"Oh, he's one of those persistent types, huh?"

"I guess so, but speaking of persistent, where's Kaliah?"

"She's home. This is your night and I didn't want any problems."

"Oh ok, well I'm glad you came."

"I wouldn't have missed this Cherish. My bad for getting mad at you for what they were doing, and I understand that their loyalty lies with you."

"It's cool. Their men are forcing them to go to the wedding, so you don't have to worry about that," I said laughing. When the song was over, I kissed him on the cheek and thanked him for the dance. As the night went on, it was actually perfect. A few kids around the neighborhood even stopped by, they were so excited that they would have a place to come to.

"Cherish, the kids are tired. I'm going to take them home now," the nanny said.

"Ok, thank you so much for coming," I said, hugging her. After placing kisses all over their faces, Mega came over and did the same exact thing, before grabbing the car seats and walking out. When he came back in, he looked as if he wanted to cry.

"Mega, what's wrong?" I asked.

"Ashley."

"What about Ashley?"

"She's gone."

"She left again?"

"No, she's dead."

"What, how?"

"I don't know everything, but Tyler just called me crying and shit."

"What are we supposed to tell Jasmine?"

"I don't know. Just when they start to really bond, this happens."

"Look, you go and find out more. I'll be there after I get rid of these people," I said.

"Are you trying to make me jealous!" Peter screamed from behind me.

"What are you talking about and lower ya voice."

"You danced with him, and now y'all having private conversations."

"Is this muthafucka serious? Didn't she dump ya ass anyways?" Mega said laughing.

"You told him our business?"

"Mega, just go, and call me when you know more," I said, ignoring Peter.

"Aight, but you sure you good?" he said, while grilling Peter.

"Yes, I'm good, now go," I said. After hugging me, he walked out of the center and I focused my attention on Peter.

"You really got some damn nerve, snapping on me like some neglected wounded dog, when I ain't even invite you here Peter, you just showed up," I said. Before Peter could speak, the mayor walked up to say his goodbyes. Looking down at my watch, I realized the party was over and everyone was leaving.

"Hey boo, you want us to wait for you?" Camille said."No, you go on home to your babies."

"Alright, love you," she said, before leaving. Soon everybody had gone and it was just me and Peter.

"Look, I'm not one of those men that's gonna just sit around waiting in the dark for you to come to your senses," he had the nerve to say.

"Me come to my senses? How about you come to yours and understand when someone is done!" I snapped.

"Just come on, let's leave and talk about this, you aren't thinking right."

"I'm thinking right, and I'm not going anywhere with you."

"Stop behaving like a child, you rode here with me."

"And I'll find a way home, believe that!"

"You know what, fuck this, I'm leaving!"

"Bye!" I snapped. Looking at me one last time, he turned and walked out of the building. Grabbing my phone, I called Mega and when he didn't answer, I called Camille, only for her phone to go straight to voicemail. Instead of trying to call anyone else, I googled a cab number and called it. After locking up the building, I headed outside to wait for the cab. As I stood outside on my phone, the last thing I remembered was everything going black.

Chapter Twenty-Two (Mega)

Pulling up to the address that Tyler texted me, I hopped out the car and there were cops everywhere. In the midst of all the chaos, I spotted the nigga Tyler in his blue uniform. Pushing past all the reporters, I walked up to him and he looked to be really going through it.

"What the fuck happened?" I asked.

"Man, this shit is crazy, come in the house," he said. Following behind him, we walked into a nice sized house, that I assumed was his.

"Now start from the beginning."

"Before I say anything, I want you to look at something for me," he said, before grabbing a DVD and placing it inside the DVD player. As soon as it started, I wasn't sure what I was looking at, until I saw a car pull up in front of the camera. I watched as Ashley got out the car and argued with someone I couldn't see. It all looked pretty innocent, until I watched someone hit her so hard, her body came crashing onto the hood of the car. As the figure beat Ashley unmercifully, the shit was so gruesome, I had to turn my head a few times.

"No, keep looking!" he snapped. Looking up at the camera, I watched as Ashley's body fell to the ground. What surprised me most was seeing Jayda's face as she wiped

Ashley's blood off of her. Picking up Ashley's body, she got inside of Ashley's car and drove off.

"Where was Ashley found?" I asked.

"Parked in front of my fucking house, in the driver's side of the car, slumped over," he said, as tears fell from his eyes.

"I'mma kill that bitch nigga!" I snapped.

"Naw, I'm handling that bitch as we speak!"

"You found her?"

"Hell yeah I found her. I wasn't always a cop, I'm a street nigga, and this bitch gotta go!"

"I can't believe that nigga beat her like she wasn't shit," I said, feeling an instant pain in my heart. I would be lying if I said I felt pain for Ashley, I really felt pain for Jasmine.

"So how you wanna handle this?" I asked.

"My niggas got her at an old warehouse, but I'mma need a team to dispose of her body. I don't need her popping up and having anything leading back to me," he said.

"I got you. I can help with that and that nigga will never be found, just call me when he's taken care of."

"Thanks. I know she was ya baby mom, but I truly loved her."

"How were you able to record that shit?" I asked.

"When I bought her the Audi, I got a dash camera installed, just in case that nigga fucked with her. I was gonna handle shit the right way and get that son of a bitch arrested, but now it's too late for that," he said sadly. After letting Tyler vent and cry, I headed home. I don't know how or when I would tell Jasmine about her mother's death, but I knew I wasn't gonna do it tonight. When I got home, Kaliah was up waiting for me and to be honest, she was the last person I wanted to deal with right now.

"How are you babe?" she asked, hugging me.

"I'm good, I just feel bad for Tyler and Jasmine."

"I understand, do they know who did it?"

"Naw, they don't have no leads. The cops think it was a robbery gone bad," I lied.

"Wow, that's so crazy. This world is such an unsafe place nowadays," she said, shaking her head.

"I just wanna go the fuck to bed," I said, not wanting to talk about Ashley anymore.

"Alright, but Ms. Evelyn called," she said.

"Is everything good?"

"Yeah, she thought Cherish was with you," she said, giving me the side eye.

Naw, I was with Ashley's dude, you already know that."

"So why would she think Cherish was with you?" she asked.

"Because I went to her grand opening," I said nonchalantly.

"Why didn't you tell me about it Jason?"

"Kaliah, I ain't doing this shit right now!"

"Doing what, I just asked a question."

"Yeah, but I know where this shit gonna lead and I ain't doing it. I just found out my baby mom was murdered by a nigga I once called my fucking best friend and you wanna be arguing about bullshit!"

"Wait, by your best friend? I thought you said it was a robbery."

"I'm going to bed, Cherish is probably with that white dude," I said before walking upstairs.

The next morning, I woke up to my phone going crazy. Rolling to my side, I grabbed it and answered it.

"Mr. Jason, Cherish still hasn't been home," she said with a worried tone.

"You sure she isn't with Peter?"

"I'm sure. I called him and he said he hasn't seen her since last night."

"And you believe him?"

"I don't know, but I'm worried."

"Did you call the police?"

"No, I wanted to talk to you first. I'm an old lady, but I ain't stupid," she said.

"I appreciate that Evelyn."

"So what you gonna do?"

"I'mma go check out that white dude, I wanna see him face to face."

"Just be careful, and don't do anything crazy. You don't have to worry about the babies, I got them," she said sweetly.

"I won't," I assured her, before hanging up. After getting dressed and ready, I called my boy that I use when I need to dig up dirt or find someone, and gave him the white dudes name. Minutes later, he called me back with an address. Grabbing my keys, I headed downstairs, only for Kaliah to stop me in my tracks.

"You leaving?"

"Yeah, I got some shit to take care of."

"Oh ok," she said sadly. Walking out the door, I hopped in my car and drove to Peter's house. When I got there, his car was parked outside. Walking up to the door, I knocked and waited for him to answer.

"Who is it!" he screamed. Instead of replying, I just stood there and waited for him to answer. When he opened the door, he was surprised to see me, and he actually seemed suspect as hell.

"Oh Jason, what are you doing at my home?" he asked nervously.

"I think you know why I'm here," I said, trying to give him room to hang himself.

"Look, I know what you're here for and I've been trying to call Cherish to apologize for what I did."

"What exactly did you do?"

"I was so angry and hurt about her ending things, that when she told me to leave, I did."

"Wait, so even though she came to the fucking party with you, ya ass left her!" I snapped. Gripping him up by his shirt, I wanted to tear his fucking head off.

"She told me to," he said, scared.

"I don't give a fuck what she told you. If she came there with you, it was your fucking job to make sure she got home!" I said, pushing him.

"Is she ok?" he asked.

"Naw, she's missing, and if anything happens to her, I swear on my kids I'll be back for ya bitch ass!" I snapped, before walking away. As I sat in my car, all I could think about was the fact that I had no clue where Cherish was. I didn't know if she was hurt, and I had no clue who could've took her, but the first thing that came to my mind was Jayda. Grabbing my phone, I called Tyler and waited for him to answer.

"Yo," he said.

"What up? My other baby mom is missing, and I need to know if you for sure have that nigga Jayden."

"I was just about to call you, my niggas picked up the wrong person. When I got to the warehouse, it was some bitch there tied up, but it wasn't that nigga."

"What the fuck, so this nigga got Cherish!"

"I'm sorry, Jason. I got my whole team looking for Jayda and I can send another team out to help you find Cherish," he said sympathetically.

"Naw, I got my own team," I said, hanging up. After hanging up on him, I called Mark.

"We got a problem, meet me at my crib," I said, before hanging up. When I got home, I sat and waited for Mark and the team to get here. If there was anyone I trusted whole heartedly to help me bring Cherish home, it was them niggas. After sitting there for a half an hour, Mark, Kasan, Chris and Terrence came walking through my basement door.

"Hello guys, would you like a drink or snacks?" Kaliah asked.

"Naw, we good."

"Alright," she said, before walking back upstairs.

"What the fuck is up?" Mark asked.

"Man, Cherish ain't come home after the party," I said, on the verge of breaking down.

"Fuck you mean she ain't come home? Has anybody heard from her?" Kasan said.

"Naw, Evelyn called all over and everybody assumed she was with that dude Peter, but I just came from there. Come to find out, they got into it and he left her."

"Damn, so where do we start?"

"I don't know, but I'm feeling real fucked up. She called last night and I was sleep," I said.

"Don't blame ya self, that shit ain't gonna bring her back."

"I think that bitch Jayda got her," I said.

"Well that's where we'll start," Kasan said, walking away to make a phone call. After calling Cherish's phone over and over, I finally gave up. I felt like someone had literally kicked me in the chest. The thought of losing Lil Mama was too hard to bare.

"We're gonna find her, but do me a favor and don't tell Camille or the other girls, she don't need to be dealing with this kinda of stress," Mark said. After making phone calls, we all headed upstairs to leave.

"Jason, what's going on?" Kaliah asked.

"Nothing."

"Don't lie to me, I know something is wrong!"

"Cherish is missing," I said.

"Oh my God, did you call the police?" she asked.

"Naw, I'mma handle it."

"Jason, what the fuck, this is a job for the police!" she snapped.

"Damn, for once, just shut up and stop questioning me!" I snapped.

"Why do you need to handle this? You acting like she's your woman, why you gotta save her?" she said sadly.

"Yo, you sound fucking stupid. She's the mother of my fucking kids, that's why I have to save her."

"You love her?" she asked.

"I never stopped, and that ain't never gonna change," I said before walking out the door.

Chapter Twenty-Three (Cherish)

Waking up, I had the biggest headache. I felt like I'd just gotten hit by a truck, my body was killing me. Opening my eyes didn't help me at all because they had my eyes covered, my mouth taped and my hands tied to what seemed to be a bedpost. Laying in the bed, I moved around, trying to get my hands out of the tight rope, but nothing was working. Out of breath and mentally tired, I stopped trying to fight and just laid there. While trying to think of a way to get out of there, I heard a door open and footsteps.

"This bitch is sexy!" I heard a man say.

"We ain't come here for that!" a female said. When I heard her voice, I instantly knew who it was.

"Whatever. I'm going out to handle business, don't untie her and don't talk to her!" he snapped.

"Ok, but when are you gonna contact them about the money?" the female said.

"Bitch, don't question me!" he snapped, before I heard the door close. I wasn't sure how long I'd been there, but my mouth was dry as hell and my stomach was cramping. With my mouth gagged, I started screaming as loud as I could, in hopes of someone hearing me. "Why you screaming?" Jayda asked. The moment I went to scream again, I started coughing hard and I couldn't stop, my throat was burning. As I coughed, I felt her lift my head up and untie the gag, before pulling it away from my mouth.

"Helppppppp!" I screamed, before she covered my mouth with her hand.

"I'm not even supposed to be in here, let alone untying you, so I need you to be quiet," she said.

"Why are you doing this, I'm not even with Jason anymore!" I pleaded. Ignoring me, she walked away from me and I heard the door close. When she came back, she lifted my head up and attempted to give me something to drink, but all I could think was that the drink was poisoned, so I closed my mouth tight.

"I'm not trying to hurt you. It's just water, I swear," she said. I knew I couldn't trust her, but at that point, what choice did I have. Opening my mouth, I let her give me the water.

"Thank you," I said.

"You're welcome, but I have to gag you again before Daddy comes."

"Your daddy?"

"I already said too much."

"No wait, don't leave me in this room alone," I pleaded.

"I'm not supposed to be talking to you," she said.

"Is he gonna kill me?" I asked.

"You took someone from us, and now you have to die," she said.

"Jayda, is this about Mega? I told you we aren't together, so who did I take?"

"Why do you keep calling me Jayda?" she asked.

"You're not Jayda?" I asked, confused. I waited for the person to reply, but instead, they got up and walked out. I knew for a fact that Jayden didn't have any other siblings, but who else could it be. A few minutes later, she came back in and tied my mouth back up. I tried to talk to her, but she refused to answer me. As I laid on the bed, I thought about my babies and how much I loved them, how much they needed me and how much I needed them. I knew that my family was looking for me. It ain't a chance in hell that Camille would be ok with not hearing from me.

"Daddy said I can't take you to the bathroom, but I can't handle the smell anymore," I heard the girl say. I couldn't respond because my mouth was covered, but I nodded my head and waited for her to untie me. I was embarrassed because just a few hours ago, I had pissed on myself for the sixth time. When she untied me, she walked me to the bathroom. I could feel the gun pointed at my back, but tired of being scared, I took the blindfold off my face. I was surprised to see standing in front of me a child who looked to be thirteen years old. She was a beautiful little white girl, who seemed lost and confused. I couldn't pinpoint her face, she didn't look familiar to me at all.

"Put your mask back on!"

"I just wanna know why you're doing this," I said.

"I didn't wanna do this, but Daddy gets mad when I say no," she said.

"Well why is he doing this?"

"You took something from my sister, and Daddy says you have to go."

"Who's your sister?"

"I can't tell you!" she screamed, before pacing the floor with the gun pointed at me.

"Calm down, please. We don't have to talk about your daddy or sister."

"You mean it?" she asked.

"I mean it, tell me about you," I said. Walking back to the room, she tied me back to the bed, but kept my blindfold and gag off.

"My name is Blue. Daddy says he named me that because of my beautiful blue eyes."

"That's a beautiful name," I said.

"Thank you," she said shyly.

"So how old are you?" I asked.

"I don't know."

"You don't know how old you are?" I asked shocked.

"I never had a birthday."

"Wow, every child deserves a birthday, Blue," I said, feeling bad for her.

"Daddy tries his hardest. I don't want to make him angry, so I don't say anything," she said, while biting her fingernails.

"I understand, so does your sister get birthdays?"

"She is his special girl, so she gets everything, she even gets to leave."

"Oh ok, are you happy with your daddy?" I said.

"Sometimes I am, but mostly I'm sad and scared."

"Well I have a place for you to go, if you ever want to leave."

"Why would you help me?"

"Because I understand you are a good girl in a bad situation."

"I don't know, what if he finds me?"

"I won't let him hurt you."

"No, no I can't!" she said, before standing up and covering my eyes and mouth back up and walking out the room.

Chapter Twenty-Four (Mega)

I hadn't been able to sleep since finding out that Lil Mama was missing. Jasmine had been asking about her, the twins were crying for her and I didn't know what to tell them.

"Daddy?"

"Hey baby girl, come here," I said, pulling her towards me.

"Have you heard from Mommy yet?" she asked.

"No, but don't worry," I said, kissing her cheek.

"Is Mommy Ashley gone forever?"

"Why would you say that?"

"Ms. Kaliah said that God took her to be with him." "She told you what!"

"It's ok daddy, don't be mad, just please find mommy. I don't want her to die too," she said, crying as she laid on my chest.

"Jasmine, I'm gonna find ya mom, but I need you to go get dressed," I said. When she was ready, I grabbed my keys and walked downstairs.

"Jason, can we talk?" Kaliah asked.

"Can this wait until later, I was about to head out and meet up with the crew," I said, not feeling her ass. Giving Jasmine a look, she knew exactly what I wanted her to do. Handing her the car keys, I turned and looked at Kaliah.

"You haven't said two words to me in two days. I understand that Cherish is missing, but I don't understand why you're making such a big deal out of it. How do you know she didn't just run off?" she asked.

"Cherish wouldn't do no shit like that. She loves our children, she wouldn't just leave them."

"Look, all I'm saying is that Cherish is barely legal and has so much responsibility, how do you know that she just isn't overwhelmed and in need of a break?"

"Because I know her and she wouldn't have handled it by running."

"You have a fiancé and children that need you right now, but you're out on some wild goose chase!" she snapped.

"Speaking of children, how the fuck you gon tell Jasmine about her mama? That wasn't your muthafucking place!" I snapped.

"What the fuck is wrong with you? Like I told you before, I'mma do whatever it takes to find Lil Mama!"

"You weren't gonna tell her and she needed to know."

"My daughter is already dealing with enough. I was gonna tell her when I decided the time was right. You got life fucked up if you think that shit was cool. Her fucking mother is missing and you tell her that her other mother is dead!"

"That's the problem, you're so worried about your precious Lil Mama that you're saying fuck everything and everybody else. I'm trying to plan our fucking wedding alone because even when you're here, you're not here!" she screamed.

"Kaliah, I don't have time for this right now!" I said, pacing the floor.

"You never have time," she said, before walking away. Walking out the door I hopped in my car and after dropping Jasmine off with Evelyn, I drove to Mark's house. When I got there, I knocked on the basement door and was met by all my niggas and their main priority was getting Cherish home safely.

"I don't understand how we can't find one fucking bitch!" I snapped.

"Man, I don't even know," Mark said. Cherish had been missing for forty-six hours and we still have no leads as to where Jayden was.

"We need to find Cherish, before something bad happens," I said, stressed.

"What you mean find Cherish?" Camille asked.

"Babe, what you doing up, go back to bed," Mark said.

"No, I'm fine, tell me what's going on!" she snapped.

"Everything is fine, we got it handled," Kasan said.

"Nigga shut up, I wasn't talking to you, I'm talking to my husband!"

"Come on Cam, calm down, that shit ain't good for the baby."

"Don't tell me to calm down, I ain't a fucking child. If something is wrong with my fucking friend, I want to know now!"

"Fuck it, just tell her," Mark said.

"Cherish is missing, we think Jayden took her."

"Nooooo! Noo, we gotta find her!" she said, as tears fell from her eyes.

"We gonna find her Cam, I promise!" Mark said, hugging her.

"How the fuck did this happen? I swear she can't catch a break. I'm so tired of muthafuckas fucking with her!" she snapped.

"Don't worry, Jayden gonna fucking pay with his life!" I snapped.

"Did y'all try to find her phone?" she asked.

"What you mean find her phone?"

"If her phone is on, then you can find it on google."

"That's some CIA, FBI shit. I told y'all the fucking government watches us all," Chris said.

"Nigga, shut the fuck up!" Kasan said, shaking his head.

"Let me go grab my laptop," she said, before rushing out. When she came back downstairs with her laptop in tow, she quickly accessed Cherish's phone, which surprised the shit out of me.

"It says she's in Burlington, NJ. Why would Jayden have her there?" she said.

"I don't know, but I'm bout to find out!" I said.

"Yeah, let's go!" Camille said.

"You ain't going nowhere, not with my baby in you!" Mark snapped.

"Well I ain't gonna just sit here while my friend is missing!"

"You did enough, now go sit ya ass down somewhere!"

"Whatever, y'all better bring my friend back in one fucking piece!" she snapped, before walking back upstairs.

After writing down the address, we loaded into the car and headed out to Burlington. Pulling up to the address, it seemed to be a normal house, nothing out of the ordinary. "We gonna stay here until it's dark, then we'll move," I said. We sat in the car and watched the house for hours, and it seemed like every few minutes, Kaliah would call me and text me, wanting to know where I was, but I ignored every call and text. At about 6pm, the sun had started to go down and right when we were about to jump out the car, cops swarmed the house. Everything happened so fast, I wasn't even sure how the fuck the cops found the place. The moment I heard a gunshot, I raced out the car, only to be stopped by police officers.

"What the fuck, my wife is in there!" I snapped. I wasn't trying to hear shit they were saying, and I continued to try and push past them.

"Jason, we have everything under control," Tyler said, surprising me.

"Man, who the fuck got shot, where is my fucking girl!" I snapped. I didn't care about what he thought he had under control. Until I laid eyes on my Lil Mama, I wouldn't be calm.

"Step over here with me, let me holla at you." Tyler said pulling me to the side.

"Man I ain't got time for this shit, I need to know what the fuck is going on!" I snapped.

"Cherish is fine, she wasn't harmed, I don't know who the fuck that nigga is or what the fuck is going on, I grabbed Jayda last night, that bitch is a done deal, I handled her my fucking self."

"Where was that nigga, and if it was him that grabbed her then who?"I asked.

"Man I don't know, but I know it was Jayda, this bitch was laid up in some hospital all beat the fuck when I found her, I went to the county to talk to the nigga that was charged and he said he didn't know that she use to be a man."

"I knew that shit was gonna catch up to his ass." I said shaking my head.

"Mega!" I heard Cherish scream. Pushing past everyone, I rushed to her and when she fell into my arms, I didn't want to let her go. As I looked over her body to make sure she was untouched, I let out a sigh of relief.

"Are you ok?" I asked, hugging her.

"You came for me?"

"Why wouldn't I, you know I always got ya back Lil Mama."

"I just thought..." she started to say, before breaking down. Picking her up, I carried her to the car. As soon as I sat her down, Camille, Shante, Shana and Queesha came running up to us.

"What the fuck are y'all doing here!" Kasan snapped.

"We had to make sure our girl was ok. I got my baby tucked away real nice," Camille said.

"You always tryna shoot somebody," Cherish said laughing.

"Excuse me, but she can't leave. She needs to be checked and we need a statement," a cop said, stopping us from leaving.

"Nigga, you need to move, I ain't leaving without her!" I snapped.

"No one knows exactly what happened in there," the cop said. Just as I was about to talk, a little girl was being brought out of the house in handcuffs. She looked so young and I didn't understand what all this was about.

"Where are y'all taking her!" Cherish jumped up.

"What's wrong, ain't she one of the people who took you?" I asked, confused.

"Nooo, she saved my life!" Cherish screamed, before running over to the girl and hugging her. At this point, I was completely fucking lost. I had no idea what was going on as she embraced this little girl. Walking up to Cherish, the little girl looked up at me and at that moment, I felt like I'd seen her before, but I couldn't figure out where.

Chapter Twenty-Five (Cherish)

"Take your time and tell us exactly what you remember," Tyler said.

"Me and Blue were talking and I was letting her know that if she let me go that I would do everything in my power to protect her from that man. She was about to let me go, when he came back to the house. She quickly tied my blindfold back on and when he walked in, he had a gun. He started rambling on about how I had tried to take someone that didn't belong to me anymore, but I had no clue what he was talking about. Before I knew what was happening, he had the gun aimed at my head, but before he could pull the trigger, Blue shot him in the chest. Seconds later, y'all came busting through the door," I said honestly. As I recalled the events, I couldn't help but cry. I was so blessed to come out of that with just a few scratches because it could've been a lot worse. As Mega held me in his arms while I was telling the story, for the first time in a long time, I felt complete.

"Did he say anything to you before passing?" Tyler asked.

"I don't remember."

"It's fine, that's all we need for right now, but I have your number."

"So what's gonna happen to Blue?"

"Right now, she will be handed over to our social worker and laced in a home."

"She can stay at my outreach program."

"Cherish, are you sure?" Mega asked.

"Yes, I'm positive. That girl ain't his child. I don't know who she belongs to, but until y'all find her actual family, then she can stay in my care."

"That's fine. You have a government funded program, so it shouldn't be a problem," Tyler said.

"Thank you, can I go now?"

"You're free to go, and I'm so sorry about what you've been through," he said. When we were done, Mega drove me home so I could be with my babies. I felt so weird because I knew we had a lot to talk about pertaining to us, but I was so mentally exhausted, I just wanted to go home.

"Do you need me to stay?" he asked.

"No, I'm sure you're just as tired as I am." "You know I love you, right?"

"Jason, please don't do this right now. You have a whole fiancé," I said, on the verge of tears.

"And I'm sorry about that, but I'mma figure this shit out," he said, before kissing my head and walking away. I knew who I wanted and where I wanted to be, but I didn't want to push what I wanted on him. I needed him to want me, not because he felt sorry, but because I'm the only woman he wanted. As soon as I got home, I kissed my sleeping babies and hopped into the shower. After spending over an hour washing off the filth, I curled up in bed. The next morning, I was awakened to the best sounds I'd ever heard in my life, crying babies and cartoons. Jumping out of bed, I walked out into the living room

"Mommyyyyy!" Jasmine said, hugging me.

"Hey baby, I missed you so much!" I said, kissing her.

"I missed you too. Daddy promised he would bring you home."

"Did he?" I asked with a smile.

"Yup!"

"You want some pancakes?" I asked.

"Yes please, chocolate chip!" she said happily. After fixing breakfast, I had to head out to the outreach program and make sure I had a room set up for Blue.

"Hey Cherish, glad to have you back!" one of my counselors said.

"Glad to be back. I have a newbie coming soon, so can you set up a room? Make sure it has the works."

"Will do," she said, before walking away. Walking into my office, I called Tyler to see what was going on with Blue and when she would be coming. Pulling out his card, I dialed his cellphone number and waited for him to answer.

"Hello?"

"Hey Tyler, I'm calling to see when Blue will be coming."

"We are on our way to you right now," he said.

"Ok, thank you so much," I said, before hanging up. After waiting ten minutes, in walked Tyler and Blue. She seemed so withdrawn and it broke my heart.

"Cherish!" she said with a smile, before hugging me.

"Hey sweety, how are you?"

"I'm ok, I kinda miss Daddy," she said, making my stomach turn.

"I understand, but don't worry, you'll be fine," I said with a smile. Walking her to her room, I was surprised by how happy she was with it.

"Wow, this is all mine?" she asked.

"Yeah, this is all yours, for as long as you want it. I'mma go talk with Mr. Tyler, you can go look around," I said, before walking out her room. Leading Tyler back to my office, I wasted no time asking questions.

"So have you heard anything?"

"No, I haven't found any of her family. But the guy who kidnapped you, we went by his house and it was extremely disturbing. His wife was also charged with child endangerment after she willingly admitted to knowing that he had kidnapped you."

"But why did he do it?" I asked. I was completely over being kidnapped and it just happened yesterday. What was eating me up was the not knowing. I mean who did I hurt so bad that they would want me dead.

"I'm still trying to figure that out, but when I do, don't worry, you will hear from me."

"I'm sorry about Ashley. At one point we had our problems, but I could see the change in her and she didn't deserve to die."

"Thank you. I miss her and I'm in pain, but I will heal," he said, before shaking my hand and walking out. As I continued to handle paperwork and introduce myself to the children, Camille and the girls walked in.

"Tell me why I went to the house to see you, only to have Ms. Evelyn tell me that you're here," Camille said.

"I can't let one monkey stop the show, I still got shit to do," I said.

"You better talk that shit!" Shante said.

"How you feeling though?" Camille asked.

"I'm ok, I'm just glad Blue is fine," I said.

"I can't believe that nigga got away with kidnapping a fucking little girl and nobody was looking for her," Queesha said, shaking her head.

"Yeah, it's crazy," Shana said.

"Alright, well how long you gonna be here?" Camille asked.

"I was about to leave before y'all came."

"Oh aight, well come on, I'm starving," Camille's pregnant ass said.

"Girl, I'm tired. I'm going home with my babies and going to bed."

"Whatever, what's up with you and Mega?" Shante asked.

"What you talkin bout?"

"Don't play stupid. We all saw how that nigga was holding his Lil Mama," Camille said.

"He is about to get married, so ain't nothin up with us."

"Whatever, be in denial all you want, but we out," Shante said before they all left.

Chapter Twenty-Six (Mega)

As I laid in bed, I couldn't get the little girl's face out my head. It was fucking me up because for the life of me, I couldn't remember where I had saw her at. As I continued to stare into the dark ceiling, it was as if a light bulb went off in my head. I jumped out of bed, grabbing my phone, and called Tyler.

"I know where I know that little girl from," I said when he answered.

"Where?"

"I went to Kaliah's parents house, and she was in a book of photos he had."

"Wait, Kaliah's father?"

"Yeah, I assumed the picture was old, but obviously not."

"So are you saying that the man who tried to kill Cherish is somehow connected to Kaliah? I ran a check on him and they never had kids."

"Can you send me a picture of the dude?" "Yeah, give me a minute," he said. When I finally got the picture, I opened it and was shocked. It was definitely the dude that Kaliah introduced to me as her dad.

"I don't know what the fuck is going on, but that's Kaliah's dad."

"Damn, this shit is fucking weird. I need some time to do some digging, give me until tomorrow afternoon," he said before hanging up. As I laid in bed, I watched as Kaliah slept and all I could think about was whether or not I actually knew the woman I was engaged to. I continued to be caught in my thoughts, until sleep took over.

The next morning, I woke up bright and early, hoping that Tyler had some news for me. I had been spending most of my time with Cherish and the kids, but every time I came home, Kaliah drove me crazy, talking about this wedding that I didn't even want. I had been trying hard to tell Kaliah that I didn't want to get married, but every time I made an attempt to tell her, she didn't give me a chance. When I came home and told her that we had found Cherish, she was disappointed and I knew why. Kaliah knew that as hard as I tried to fight it, my heart belonged to Cherish. At the same time, I felt fucked up for hurting Kaliah.

"Hey babe, I'm so glad things are back to normal," Kaliah said, kissing me.

"Yeah, me too," I said.

"So I've been thinking maybe we should just go to city hall. I mean I don't have anyone to bring, so it would be small anyways."

"When?"

"We can go right now!"

"I don't know, Kaliah."

"We gotta talk Jason," she said, sitting on my lap.

"Alright, what's up?"

"I'm pregnant. I know you weren't trying to have a child right now, but I don't want to give birth without being married."

"You're pregnant, but how?" I said, confused. I mean damn, I thought my pull out game was strong, but I know there was always a possibility of it happening.

"Well we weren't using condoms Jason," she said.

"I know Kaliah but..." I started to finish, but was interrupted by my ringing phone.

"Hello?"

"Are you sitting down?" Tyler asked.

"Yeah, what's up?"

"Man, this shit is crazy. Well I found out that Kaliah was kidnapped by that couple almost thirty years ago. The police found her, but she refused to leave the couple and would run back to their house every chance she got."

"Damn, they fucked her up," I said as I stared at Kaliah.

"Before you go feeling sorry for her, there's more. I retrieved his phone records and he has several phone calls from Kaliah on the night she was kidnapped," he said. Getting up, I walked out into my office and closed the door.

"Yeah, but that was her father. Isn't it normal that she would call him?"

"We also retrieved text messages and it isn't looking good. She sent him the address to the outreach program, twenty minutes before Cherish was taken."

"Get the fuck outta here!" I screamed.

"Calm down, I don't want her to know that we know."

"You need to come get this bitch asap before I kill her." "I'm on my way, don't be stupid," he said, before hanging up. Walking back into the living room, I watched as Kaliah looked through wedding magazines, as if she didn't have a care in the world.

"Oh good, you're off the phone," she said with a smile.

"Yeah."

"So about the baby, I was thinking if it's a boy, we can name him Jayson," she said.

"I already have a Jr., Kaliah."

"I know, which is why we'll add a Y to his name and change it up," she said with a smile.

"What the fuck is wrong with you Kaliah!"

"Ok, calm down, I'll think of another name."

"Tell me why you did it!"

"Did what?"

"Why the fuck would you try and kill Cherish!" I screamed.

"I can explain!" she pleaded.

"Ain't no explaining that shit, that girl ain't never did shit to you!"

"She did everything to me, but you're too fucking blind to see it!"

"You're fucking crazy!"

"She took Jasmine. That girl would've loved me if she didn't have Cherish feeding her bad shit about me. She took your friends from me, they hated me because she hated me. And she was working on taking you. You think I was gonna let her continue to ruin our relationship!" she screamed. Grabbing her neck, I tried to choke the life out of her. As her legs dangled in the air, I could feel my hands taking her life.

"Let her go!" I heard Tyler scream.

"This bitch is crazy!" I snapped.

"She'll be charged, she'll never bother you again!" he screamed. As I continued to choke her, I thought about Cherish and my babies and I realized this crazy bitch wasn't worth it. Letting her drop to the ground, I walked away from her.

"Jasonnnnnnnn, please don't leave. I didn't want to hurt her, this is your fault!" she screamed, causing me to stop in my tracks.

"My fault?" I asked.

"You knew you didn't love me. You used me to try to get over that bitch, but I loved you with everything in me. I thought maybe I was just tripping, but when I saw the way she looked at you on the news, I knew she had to go."

"On the news?"

"Yeah, her little grand opening. She spoke so highly of you, and then you lied about going. After searching through ya shit, I found out that she invited both of us!" she screamed. I couldn't do shit but shake my head.

"Why couldn't you love me like you loved her? I tried to do everything to keep you happy, but nothing worked because I could never be her!" she screamed. Turning away from her, I walked away and out of my house. Getting into my car as I drove away, I could hear her screaming my name. Pulling up to Cherish's house, I got out the car and banged on her door as hard as I could. When she opened it, she looked at me with wide eyes. Grabbing her, I kissed her the way I wanted to since the day we broke up. We'd made so many mistakes, wasted so much time arguing and hating each other, that we forgot how much we loved each other.

"I'm sorry Lil Mama," I said in between kisses.

"I'm sorry too, I was being so childish," she said. Covering her mouth with mine, I shut her up. Picking her up into my arms, I carried her to her bedroom and laid her on the bed. Removing her clothes, I looked at her body and I knew that her body was the last one I would see for the rest of my life. Her lips were the last lips I would ever kiss, her skin was the last that I would ever touch. As much as we wanted to hate each other, we never could because we were always connected and destined.

"What are we doing?" Cherish asked.

"I love you Lil Mama. I want to spend the rest of my life with you. If you don't feel the same way, tell me now, but if you do, then marry me," I said.

"What about Kaliah?"

"That bitch crazy!" I said, before telling her everything.

"Damn, Camille called that shit. She always knew the bitch was a weirdo."

"I'm so sorry I didn't see it, and I'm sorry about what she tried to do."

"I'm over being angry, now I just wanna be happy."

"I promise I'll never hurt you again, I just need you to trust me."

Chapter Twenty-Seven (Cherish)

It has been a few months since everything happened, and me and Mega have never been happier. We decided to take our time and date for a while, before jumping into anything too quickly. I feel like that was our biggest mistake. I was young and going through a lot and from the moment I met him, he was my protector and savior. Even though we're taking it slow, we haven't been able to keep our hands off each other.

"Have you decided what you're gonna do?" he asked, shaking me out my thoughts.

"You mean, what *we're* gonna do?"

"Yeah, aight. I mean you don't wanna come home and it's too small for us all to stay here."

"I'm not gonna bring me and the kids into a house that you shared with the next bitch!"

"I got a new bed."

"Don't make me slap ya ass. Plus, is that crazy chick still sending you letters?"

"Yeah, she's still claiming to be pregnant with my baby."

"I'm gonna go see her."

"Why would you do that?"

"I'm just wanna see for myself. If she is pregnant, she should be showing."

"So what happens if she is?"

"Mega, if that girl is pregnant, then we'll handle it. I mean it isn't like I didn't know y'all were fucking. I mean shit, you proposed."

"I know, but part of me feels like if she actually is pregnant, then that would fuck up everything we've been working on and set us back."

"Mega, I wasted too much time being miserable without you, just to prove a point. Whatever happened while we were apart doesn't matter," I said, kissing him.

"I think we should take a vacation from all this bullshit."

"I don't know Mega. With the outreach program and the kids, I don't know if I have time to be going on vacation." "You have employees that know what they're doing, and we have Ms. Evelyn to handle the kids. You've been through so much and I think you need a break," he said. Maybe he was right, I had been stretching myself pretty thin.

"Alright, we can plan something."

"Bet! I'll handle everything and all you have to do is show up when I call."

"I hear you babe," I said laughing. This nigga never planned anything without my help. Birthday parties, presents for the kids, he never could do anything by himself. I knew he wanted to do it and surprise me because deep down, Mega was romantic, but I honestly didn't think he could pull it off.

"What you gotta do today?" he asked.

"I have a doctor's appointment."

"Oh, you gonna go get that dumb ass shit stuck up in you," he said with an attitude.

"Jason, don't start ya shit. I don't want any more kids right now so yes, I'm gonna get this birth control. You just need to be happy that it will only last five years."

"You acting just like Camille, like you don't wanna have no babies with the nigga you love."

"I wanna have more babies, just not right now. If you respect me, then I need you to understand and respect that."

"Whatever. So is that all you're doing?"

"Yup, then I'mma head into the office for a lil," I said, before getting dressed. After I was dressed and ready, I gave my babies kisses and headed out.

The drive to Ancora Psychiatric Facility was only thirty minutes long. When I got there, they gave me a name tag, checked my pockets and even made me take off my earrings and any other potentially dangerous items, before letting me back. Sitting at the table, I waited for Kaliah to come and when she came walking out, I felt relieved to see her flat stomach.

"What are you doing here?" she asked.

"I just wanted to come here and get some answers, like I told you in the letter."

"What do you want to know, why I did it? The answer is simple."

"What did I ever do to you for you to want me dead?" I asked. These were questions I wished I could ask everyone who did me wrong, but they were no longer here. The worst feeling in the world is not knowing and I refused to live that way.

"I tried to be your friend, but you didn't want that."

"You were with my kids' father, the love of my life, what made you think that I would ever want to be your friend Kaliah?"

"Jason wanted so bad to be in love with me, but he couldn't do that with you in the picture. I thought he could, but he wasn't strong enough."

"Why did you lie about being pregnant?"

"I knew he was gonna leave me, desperate times call for desperate measures," she said with a laugh.

"So all of this was about getting Jason?"

"What, you thought it was about you? It was never about you Cherish, you are nothing to me. I just wanted what you had, the kid, Jason, the life. You had all this right in your fucking face, but you didn't want it, so why not just give it to me? I could've been a great you, I could've made Jason and the kids so happy."

"I always wanted my life, I was just too young to know it. You could have never been me, I mean face it, there is only one Cherish Daniels, and it ain't you. You tried so hard to be me that you stopped being yourself. For a moment I liked you, hell, I was almost even jealous of you, but if you taught me one thing, it's to go hard and don't look back. Don't worry, I'mma love Jason and ride with that nigga until the wheels fall off," I said, before getting up and attempting to walk out, only for her to pull me back and kiss me.

"I thought it was Jason, but it's you Cherish," she said. I had to do a double take, was this bitch really gazing into my eyes? As the guards swarmed her, she was still staring at me with a crazed look in her eyes. I couldn't do shit but shake my head as I walked out, never once looking back. Some people do things for a reason and other do things simply because they're a few chapters short of a fucking book. I now knew that even when Kaliah seemed cool, she was always crazy, she just did a better job at hiding it than most. Getting into my car, I drove straight past the doctor's office. The truth is, I don't want any more kids and the moment me and Peter started getting serious, I took my ass to the doctor and got on birth control. I didn't think Mega needed to know that I was planning on sleeping with Peter, so I left out a lot of information. We all know women handle things better than men, so certain shit we just need to take to the grave. Before I could make it into work, Jason called me, letting me know to meet him at the house. Pulling up into my driveway, I hopped out the car, only to have Jason rush me into his.

"Babe, what are you doing?" I asked.

"Just sit back, shut up and don't ask any questions," he said, turning me on. As he drove closer to the airport, I couldn't help but smile.

"Mega, I didn't even pack anything."

"What I say!" he snapped, shutting my ass up. When we arrived at the airport, he handed me a blindfold.

"Uh huh, I ain't putting this shit on my face," I said. I wasn't trying to be difficult, but I still wasn't over being kidnapped, and the last thing I wanted was something tied on my eyes.

"Do you trust me Lil Mama?"

"You know I do."

"I need you to trust me enough to know that I would never let anything happen to you," he said, kissing me softly, before placing the blindfold on my eyes. When we boarded the plane, he waited until we were in the air, before he took the blindfold off.

"We going to Jamaica!" I said happily.

"Yeah, I said fuck the Bahamas since you went there with that lame ass dude," he said with a smirk.

"Shut up!" I said laughing. After hours of flying and two planes later, we were finally in Jamaica and I couldn't be more in awe by how beautiful it was.

"Come on babe, you gotta get dressed so we can be out," Mega said, rushing me.

"Boy bye, I'm tired as hell, I'm going to go lay down," I said.

"I have a surprise for you though babe," he said. When we got to our room on the beach, he wasted no time pushing me towards the shower. After washing off all the plane funk, I turned the water off and covered up with a towel. Walking out of the bathroom, Mega was nowhere to be found.

"He didn't even bring luggage," I said to myself as I stood there, naked as hell. Walking into the bedroom, I saw the most beautiful mermaid dress that I'd ever seen in my life. After getting dressed, I walked into the living room to grab my phone, only to run into Mega, kneeling down on one knee.

"I love you with all my heart and soul. I know we rushed into this at the beginning, but now there is no doubt in my mind that you are who I want to spend the rest of my life with. I don't want to go another day without you having my last name, so I need you to marry me," he said. As tears fell from my eyes, I thought about all we'd been through, all the pain and disappointment we caused each other, but then I thought about not having him in my life and the decision was easy. Placing the engagement ring on my finger, he walked me downstairs and onto the beach. I could see people standing there, but I wasn't sure who they were. As we got closer, I spotted Camille, Shante, Shana, Queesha, all of their men, my babies, Ms. Evelyn, Mama Betty and her boyfriend. As I stood surrounded by the people that loved me the most, the tears continued to pour. "You look beautiful," Camille said, hugging me. I didn't have on any makeup, just a little lip gloss, but I knew in my heart that I didn't need any of that. Not today, because the man I was marrying loved me just the way I was. As I stood in front of Jason with my hand in his, I felt his love radiating onto me.

"Before we get started on your vows, Jasmine wrote something she wanted to share," the man prepared to marry us said.

"Mommy, I love you so much. I always thought that babies only had one mommy, but now I know that the real special ones get two. You love me every day and you spend time with me and take me to the park and when I'm sad you make everything all better. I'm glad that you and Daddy are happy again because I missed our family. Ummmmmm, that's all I had to say," she said with a smile that brightened my day. Bending down, I hugged and kissed her, while telling her how much I loved her, before standing back up.

Dear Lil Mama,

From the moment I laid eyes on you, I felt an instant connection, a need to protect you and be everything you needed me to be. Who would've thought that the connection would lead to me falling in love with this quiet, lost and beautiful girl. Some people go a lifetime without finding the person genuinely made for them, so when you're one of those lucky few to find that one true love, you don't let it go, you don't procrastinate and you don't fuck up. I had you, I lost you and now I've been blessed to have to you again. Best believe I ain't never letting you go," he said. I was so happy I didn't have on any make-up because the way my eyes were leaking, it would have worked out.

"I didn't write anything. Y'all know this was a surprise, but I'mma speak from my heart," I said.

"You go head, baby!" Mama Betty said, causing me to laugh.

"My king, my hero, my everything, when I met you, I was lost, battered and broken. I was at the verge of giving up and I prayed to God every day to save me. I was a good person, I was nice to people, so why wasn't I being heard? I thought maybe he was so busy helping others that he just hadn't gotten to my prayers yet, but I continued to pray and he sent me you. He chose someone persistent enough to love me, no matter how much I pushed them away. He found someone crazy enough to love all my flaws and shortcomings. I'm difficult, strong willed, sometimes mean, and sometimes I get sad for no reason at all. I'm stubborn as a bull, but you guys all know that already. It takes a strong man to deal with a broken woman, but you handle it without breaking a sweat and I love you for that. We've been through so much in such a short period of time, but no matter what battles we had to fight, we always found our way back to each other. I love you with every piece of my being, and I'm excited and humbled to be marrying the love of my life today. I can't wait to get on your nerves for the rest of your life," I said.

"Do you, Jason Cruz, take Cherish Daniels to be your wife, do you vow to love her in good times and in bad, in sickness and in health for as long as you both shall live?" "I do!" Jason screamed.

"Do you Cherish Daniels, take Jason Cruz to be your husband, do you vow to love him in good times and in bad, in sickness and in health for as long as you both shall live?"

"I do," I said with a smile.

"I now pronounce you two man and wife, you may now kiss your bride," he said. Grabbing my face, he kissed me as if it was the last time we would ever kiss again.

Eight Years Later

Sometimes bad things have to happen before the good can come. Sometimes you have to have your heart broken, so that when the real thing comes, you can truly appreciate it. I have been through so much in my life. I have been raped and beaten, mistreated and betrayed. I thought that I would never find someone to love me, I thought I didn't deserve a family. My mother told me I wasn't shit so much that I believed her, and to this day, I'm still working on healing the damage my mother caused. Every day I'm healing more and more with the love of good friends, an amazing husband, and beautiful children. I'm seeing more and more every day that God had plans for me all along, I just had to wait my turn.

"Lil Mama, you better get your daughter before I whoop her ass!" Mega said, sounding pissed.

"What's the problem?"

"Nothing, Daddy just mad. I's bad enough I chose a school in Jersey, but now he trippin tryna get me to still live at home and not at the dorms," Jasmine said.

"Mega, you wanted Jasmine closer and she is, but you need to work with her a little bit."

"Man, you know what the fuck they do in them dorms, they party and get wasted!"

"He doesn't trust me!"

"No, I don't trust them horny niggas!" he snapped.

"Damnit Jason, we raised her right. She's an honor student and has never given us any problems, let her live!" I snapped on his ass.

"Thanks mom," Jasmine said, kissing my cheek.

"Uh huh, you wanna be all up on ya mom, I guess you don't need this new car," Mega said with keys in his hand.

"No, noooo daddy, I do!" she begged, before snatching the keys. Running outside while in her cap and gown, she hopped in her car and started the ignition.

"You better put ya seatbelt on and don't be texting or talking on that damn phone!" Jason snapped.

"Thank you so much daddy, I'mma meet y'all at graduation," she screamed, before putting on her seat belt and pulling off.

"What am I gonna do with that girl?" he said shaking his head.

"We're gonna continue to love her and you need to start trusting her," I said, shaking my head.

"Let's go twins!" he screamed, ignoring the hell out of me. I swear he had Jasmine on a short leash. I tried to tell him that if he didn't loosen up some that shit would hit the fan, but of course Mega's ass don't listen to shit. As we piled into the car, we headed to Jasmine's graduation. When we pulled up, the whole team was outside, surrounding Jasmine's car. Mylee was begging Mark for a new car since she had recently gotten her permit. Sparkle was in college out of state and couldn't make it.

"Hey girl, so you finally talked Jason's ass into getting her a car," Camille said, while pushing her twins in the stroller. Yup, Mark ass ended up knocking her up with twins a year ago, so now she had Sparkle who was twenty-three, Mylee who was sixteen, Mark who was ten, and Markese and Melissa who were one. She swore up and down she was done having kids, but with the way they were fucking, you never knew what to expect. As we all went into the school and took our seats, we waited until Jasmine was called and of course, we screamed and cheered, while she looked embarrassed.

"Yassssssss Jasmine, you better get that diploma!" Shante screamed, causing us both to laugh. Shante and Kasan got married shortly after me Mega. They still only have one son, but that's all they need since he's driving them crazy as hell. Word on the street is he's running around with some gang like he ain't got no sense. Shana and Terrence are still going strong. Her son R.J. and Mark's daughter Sparkle call themselves being engaged. Shana doesn't like it one bit, but they've been together since they were twelve, so I highly doubt it's puppy love, Shana just can't grasp the concept of her son being in love. Queesha finally lost her battle to AIDS. She fought hard, but ended up getting pneumonia and taking a turn for the worst. Chris stayed by her side up until the day she died and now has full custody of her son. He still comes around sometimes, but I think being around us just reminds him too much of her. We all to this day are the best of friends, and no matter how old we get, we still have our issues and drama, but nothing that we can't get past. Every day I thank God for blessing me with a group of friends that got my back, front and sides.

The End......... For now...

CHANDLER PARK LIBRARY
12800 Harper Ave.
Detroit, MI 48213

0 5697018()

CPSIA information can be obtained
at www.ICGtesting.com
Printed in the USA
LVHW091725291218
602155LV00001B/10/P